HOW
I BECAME
A NUN

Also by César Aira from New Directions

AN EPISODE IN THE LIFE OF A LANDSCAPE PAINTER

HOW
I BECAME
A NUN

César Aira

Translated from the Spanish by
Chris Andrews

A New Directions Paperbook Original

DR © 2005, Ediciones Era, S.A. de C.V.
Translation copyright © 2007 by Chris Andrews

Originally published by Beatriz Viterbo Editora, Argentina, as *Cómo me hice monja*, in 1993; published by arrangement with the Michael Gaeb Literary Agency, Berlin.

Manufactured in the United States of America.
New Directions Books are printed on acid-free paper.
First published as a New Directions Paperbook Original (NDP1043) in 2006
Published simultaneously in Canada by Penguin Books Canada Limited.

Library of Congress Cataloging-in-Publication Data

Aira, César, 1949-
  [Cómo me hice monja. English]
  How I became a nun / Cesar Aira ; translated from the Spanish by Chris
Andrews.
     p. cm.
  ISBN-13: 978-0-8112-1631-9 (alk. paper)
  ISBN-10: 0-8112-1631-4 (alk. paper)
  I. Andrews, Chris. II. Title.
PQ7798.1.I7C6613 2006
863'.64--dc22

                              2006030115

New Directions Books are published for James Laughlin
By New Directions Publishing Corporation,
80 Eighth Avenue, New York, New York 10011

HOW
I BECAME
A NUN

1

MY STORY, THE STORY of "how I became a nun," began very early in my life; I had just turned six. The beginning is marked by a vivid memory, which I can reconstruct down to the last detail. Before, there is nothing, and after, everything is an extension of the same vivid memory, continuous and unbroken, including the intervals of sleep, up to the point where I took the veil.

We had moved to Rosario. For the first six years of my life, Mom, Dad and I lived in the province of Buenos Aires, in a town of which I have no recollection and to which I have not returned since: Coronel Pringles. The big city (as it seemed, by contrast) made an enormous impression on us. Within a few days of our arrival, my father kept a promise he had made: to buy me an ice cream. It was to be my first, since ice cream was not to be had in Pringles. Dad, who had been to the city as a young man, had on various occasions sung the praises of this delicacy, which he remembered as a glorious treat, although he was not able to put its special charm into words. He had described it to me, quite rightly, as something the uninitiated could not imagine, and that was all it took to plant "ice cream" in my childish mind, where it grew, taking on mythic proportions.

We made our way on foot to an ice-cream store that we had noticed the previous day. In we went. Dad ordered a fifty-cent ice cream for himself, with scoops of pistachio, sweet cream, and whisky-kumquat; for me, he ordered a ten-cent cone with a single scoop of strawberry. I loved the pink color. My frame of mind was positive. I was a devoted daughter. Dad could do no wrong in my eyes. We sat down on a sidewalk bench, under the trees (there were plane trees back then in downtown Rosario). I watched how Dad was doing it; in a matter of seconds he had disposed of his scoop of green ice cream. I dipped my little spoon in with great care and lifted it to my mouth.

No sooner had the first particles dissolved on my tongue than I felt physically ill. I had never tasted anything so revolting. I was rather fussy about food and had mastered the art of feigning disgust when I didn't feel like eating, but this went beyond anything I had ever tasted; it more than justified my worst exaggerations, even the ones I had refrained from acting out. For a fraction of a second I considered pretending. Dad had set his heart on making me happy, which was unusual, given his distant, irascible nature, averse to displays of affection, so it seemed a sin to spoil the occasion. I briefly envisioned the horrific prospect of eating the whole ice cream just to please him. It was only a thimbleful, the tiniest, kiddie-size cup, but at that moment it might as well have been a ton.

I don't know if my heroism would have stretched that far, but I didn't get a chance to put it to the test. The first mouthful provoked an involuntary grimace of disgust; Dad couldn't help but see. The grimace was almost exaggerated, expressing both the physiological reaction and its accompanying emotions: disillusion, fear, and the terrible sadness of being unable to bond with my father, even in the pursuit of a simple pleasure. Trying to hide it would have been absurd; even today, I couldn't hide it if I tried, because that grimace is still there on my face.

"What's wrong?"

Everything that was going to happen was audible in his tone.

Under normal circumstances I would have burst out crying at this point and been unable to reply. Like many hypersensitive children, I was perpetually on the verge of tears. But that horrendous taste, having descended into my throat, rose again like a backlash and sent a sudden shock through my body.

"Uggh . . ."

"What?"

"It's . . . awful."

"It's what?"

"Awful!" I shrieked in desperation.

"You don't like the ice cream?"

I remembered him saying as we walked to the store, among other remarks infused with pleasant anticipation, "We'll find out if you like ice cream." Naturally he said this assuming that I would. Don't all children? Some adults even remember their childhood as little more than a perpetual begging for ice cream. Which is why there was a tone of incredulous fatalism to his question, as if to say: "I don't believe it: even in a simple thing like this you're going to let me down."

I could see the indignation and scorn building in his eyes, but he controlled himself. He decided to give me another chance.

"Eat it. It's yummy," he said, and to prove it he scooped up a spoonful from his cone and put it into his mouth.

It was too late for me to back down now. The die was cast. In a way I didn't want to back down. I was beginning to realize that my only hope, having come this far, was to prove to Dad that what he had in his hands was revolting. I looked in horror at the pink of the ice cream. Farce was beginning to impinge on reality. Worse than that: farce was becoming reality, right in front of me, through me. I felt dizzy, but there was no turning back.

"It's awful! It's sickening!" I tried to whip myself into a frenzy. "It's foul!"

He said nothing. He stared into the empty space in front of him and quickly ate his ice cream. I was obviously getting nowhere, again. So, in a panic, I changed tack abruptly.

"It's bitter," I said.

"No, it's sweet," he replied with a forced and threatening gentleness.

"It's bitter!" I shouted.

"It's sweet."

"It's bitter!!"

Dad had already given up hope of getting any satisfaction from the outing. Sharing a pleasure and a moment of companionship: it was too late for all that now, and he must have been wondering how he could have been so naïve, how he could ever have thought it possible. And yet, just to rub salt into his own wound, he set about trying to convince me of my mistake. Or to convince himself that I was *his* mistake.

"It's a very sweet strawberry-flavored ice cream—delicious."

I shook my head.

"No? So what flavor does it have then?"

"It's horrible!"

"I think it's delicious," he said calmly, gulping down another spoonful. His calmness was the most frightening thing of all.

My attempt to make peace was typically convoluted:

"I don't know how you can enjoy that junk," I said, in

what was supposed to be an admiring tone of voice.

"Everyone likes ice cream," he said, white with rage. The mask of patience was slipping, and I don't know how I managed to hold back my tears. "Everyone except you, son, because you're a moron."

"No, Dad! I swear!"

"Eat that ice cream." (Coldly, sharply.) "I bought it for you to eat, you little moron."

"But I can't . . .!"

"Eat it. Try it. You haven't even tried it."

Opening my eyes wide at this slur on my honesty (only a monster would have lied for the fun of it), I cried, "I swear it's horrible!"

"Of course it's not horrible. Try it."

"I tried it already. I can't!"

Then he had an idea. He reverted to a condescending tone. "You know what it is? The coldness gave you a shock. Not the taste, but how cold it is. You'll soon get used to that, and then you'll realize how delicious it is."

I clutched at that straw. I wanted to believe in that possibility, which would never have occurred to me in a thousand years. But deep down I knew it was hopeless. It wasn't the coldness. I wasn't accustomed to ice-cold drinks (we didn't have a freezer) but I had tried them, and I knew it wasn't the coldness. Even so, I clung to that explanation. With extreme care I took a tiny scrape of ice cream on the tip of the spoon, and mechanically raised it to my mouth.

It was a thousand times more disgusting than the first taste. I would have spat it out, if I'd known how. I've never learnt how to spit properly. It came dribbling out between my lips.

Dad had been watching my every move out of the corner of his eye, all the while eating big spoonfuls of his ice cream. The three different-colored layers were rapidly disappearing. He flattened what remained with the little spoon, making it level with the edges of the cone, which he then proceeded to eat. I didn't know that the cones were edible; to me this was an act of savagery, and it burst the banks of my fear. I began to shake. I could feel the tears welling up.

With his mouth full, he said to me, "Try it properly, idiot! A big spoonful so you can actually taste it."

"Bbb . . . but."

He finished his cone and threw the spoon on the ground. A wonder he didn't eat that too, I thought. With his hands free, he turned towards me, and I knew that the sky was falling.

"Now eat it! Can't you see it's melting?"

It was true: the peak of the ice cream was turning to liquid, and pink streams were running over the edge of the cone, dripping onto my hand and my arm, then down onto my skinny legs below the hem of my shorts. There was no way I could move now. My anxiety was mounting exponentially. Ice cream seemed the cruelest instrument of torture ever invented. Dad snatched the spoon from my other hand and dug it in. He lifted a big spoonful up to my mouth. My only defense would have been to press my lips shut and never open them again. But I couldn't. I opened my mouth wide, and in went the spoon. It came to rest on my tongue.

"Shut your mouth."

I did. Tears were already misting my vision. As my tongue pressed against my palate and I felt the ice cream dissolving, my whole body was seized by a convulsion. I didn't go through the motions of swallowing. Disgust flooded through me; it was exploding in my brain like a flash of lightning. Another big spoonful was on the way. I opened my mouth. I was already crying. Dad put the spoon in my free hand.

"Go on."

I choked, coughed, and began to wail.

"Now you're being stubborn. You're just doing it to annoy me."

"No, Daddy!" I stammered unintelligibly. It came out as, "Da no dy no no da."

"Don't you like it? Eh? Don't you like it? You're a moron, you know that?" I was crying. "Answer me. If you don't like it, that's OK. We'll just chuck it in the trash, end of story."

He said it as if the story could end there. The worst thing was that, because he had eaten his ice cream so quickly, his tongue had gone numb and he was talking in a way I had never heard him talk before, with a slur that made him fiercer, harder to understand, and much more scary. I thought his tongue had gone stiff with rage.

"Tell me why you don't like it. Everyone likes it except you. Tell me the reason."

Astonishingly, I was able to speak; but I had so little to say. "Because it's horrible."

"No, it's not horrible. I like it."

He took my arm and guided my hand, with the spoon in it, toward the ice cream.

"I don't," I implored.

"Just eat it, then we'll go. What was the point of bringing you?"

"But I don't like it. Please, please . . ."

"All right. I'll never buy you another ice cream. But you're going to eat this one."

Mechanically I dug the spoon in. I felt faint at the mere thought that this torture was going to continue. All willpower had deserted me. I was crying openly, making no attempt to hide it. Luckily we were alone. At least Dad was spared public humiliation. He was quiet now, sitting still. He was looking at me with the same deep, visceral disgust I felt, staring at my strawberry ice cream. I wanted to say something, but I didn't know what. That I didn't like the ice cream? I had already said that. That the ice cream tasted foul? I had said that too, and it was pointless, because I couldn't get it across; it was still there inside me, impossible to convey, even after I had spoken. For him, the ice cream was exquisite, because he liked it. Everything was impossible, and always would be. I buckled and broke under the weight of tears. There was no hope of any consolation. The incommunicability cut both ways. He couldn't tell me how much he despised me, how much he hated me. This time, I had gone too far. His words could not reach me.

2

AS I SAID AT THE END of the previous chapter, the conversation, if that was what it had been, was over. We had lapsed into a silence that swallowed even the sound of my fitful sobbing. My father was a statue, a block of stone. Shaken, trembling, tear-sodden, holding the ice cream cone in one hand and the spoon in the other, my red face twisted in an anxious wince, I was paralyzed too. More so in fact, since I was fastened to a pain that towered over my childhood, my smallness, and my extreme vulnerability, indicating the scale of the universe. Dad had given up. My one last, desperate hope of turning the situation around would have been to get accustomed to the taste and finish the ice cream of my own free will. But it was impossible. I didn't need to be told. I didn't even need to think about it. Utterly helpless as I was, I had a firm grip on the reins of the impossible. My sobs echoed in that empty Rosario street, shaded by plane trees, oppressed by the still January heat. The sun was doodling among the shadows. I was crying my eyes out and the ice cream was melting flagrantly now, pink rills running down to my elbow, then dripping onto my leg.

But nothing lasts forever. Something else always happens. What happened next came from my body, from deep within, without any deliberate preparation or forethought. My solar plexus was convulsed by a retch. It was grotesque, farcical. As if something inside me was trying to show that it had vast reserves of energy ready to be unleashed at any moment. And straight away, another retch, even more exaggerated. To the many layers of my fear, one more was added: fear of being possessed by an uncontrollable physical mechanism.

Dad looked at me, as if returning from somewhere very far away. "That's enough drama."

Another retch. And another. And one more. It was a series. All dry, without any vomit. It was like a car hurtling towards an abyss, slamming on the brakes. But over and over, as if the abyss kept splitting.

A look of interest appeared on Dad's face. I knew that face so well: sallow, round, the hairline receding prematurely, the aquiline nose my sister inherited, not me, and the overly wide gap between nose and mouth, which he hid with a neatly trimmed moustache. I knew it so well, I didn't have to look. He was a predictable man. For me, at least. I must have been predictable for him too. But the retching had surprised him. He looked at me almost as if I had become an object, detached from him and his destiny. Meanwhile, I was pursuing mine. Retch. Retch. Retch.

Eventually the retching abated, without having produced any vomit. I was no longer crying. I controlled myself, clinging to a sad paralysis. Another residual retch. A bilious hiccup.

"I don't believe this. Son of a bitch . . ."

He was slightly hesitant. He must have been wondering how he was going to take me home. Poor Dad, he didn't realize that he would never take me home again. Although I'm sure that if someone had told him right then, he would have been relieved.

I was still holding the cone and, what with all the retching, I was spattered with ice cream from head to foot; it was all over my clothes. So the first thing he did was to take the cone away from me; then he took the spoon from my other hand. I was very slim and petite, even for my age (I had just turned six). Dad was big without being hefty. His fingers, however (which I *have* inherited), were long and slender; delicately, they relieved me of my two burdens. He looked for somewhere to throw them. But he wasn't really looking because he hadn't taken his eyes off me. Then he did something surprising.

He put the spoon into the cone, dipped it into the

remains of the pink ice cream, half-melted now but still solid enough to scoop up, and lifted it to his mouth. I shall not slight the memory of my father by suggesting that he couldn't let an ice cream go to waste when he had paid good money for it. I'm sure that's not what it was. Sometimes he had miserly reflexes, as we all do, but not in a situation like that. He had always been a straightforward, small-town sort of guy. I'm sure he didn't even imagine the possibility of complicating the tragedy. I like to think that he did it simply to relish a spoonful, just one spoonful of delicious, genuine strawberry ice cream. Like an ultimate, secret, sublime confirmation.

But then the situation turned around. He screwed up his face in a grimace of disgust and spat emphatically. It was revolting! I was staring at him pop-eyed (I was pop-eyed already from the retching), seeing double or triple. I should have been exulting in the triumph of the weak, a sentiment I knew so well, the triumph of those for whom vindication always comes too late. And perhaps there was an element of that, since the habit was deeply ingrained. But I didn't feel exultant. In fact I didn't really understand what was going on. Instead of accepting the obvious explanation, as any person in their right mind would have done, I was so caught up in the disaster that I was looking for something more baroque, another turn of the screw that would *not* cancel out what had gone before.

He lifted the cone to his nose and gave it a good sniff. His expression of disgust intensified. There was that stalling of imperceptible movements that precedes the swing into action. He wasn't a man of action; in that respect he was normal. But sometimes action has to be taken. He didn't look at me. Throughout the rest of that ill-fated afternoon, he didn't look at me again. Although I must have been quite a sight to behold. Not once did he look in my direction. Looking would have been a kind of explaining, and it was already too late for explanation to bridge the gap between us. He got up and headed for the ice-cream store, leaving me alone on the sidewalk bench, all in a mess and crying. But I followed him.

"Mister . . ."

The ice cream vendor looked up from his comic book. He tried to compose his features, because he sensed there was a problem, but he couldn't imagine what it might be.

"This lousy ice cream you sold me is off."

"No."

"What do you mean, No, for Christ's sake!"

"No sir, all the ice cream I sell is fresh."

"Well, this one is rotten."

"What flavor is it? Strawberry? It was delivered this morning."

"What the hell do I care? It's rotten."

"Doesn't come any fresher," insisted the vendor. He looked along the row of drums with aluminum lids lined up under the counter and opened one. "Here it is. Brand new; I opened it for you."

"Don't try it out on me."

"Is it my fault if the boy didn't like it?"

Dad had gone red with fury. He held out the cone.

"Try it!"

"I don't have to try anything."

"No . . . you're going to try it and you're going to tell me if . . ."

"Don't shout at me."

In spite of this reasonable suggestion, both of them were shouting.

"I'm going to report you."

"Don't make me laugh."

"Who do you think you are?"

"Who do you think *you* are?"

By this stage it had become a battle of wills. It was too late for the problem to be solved in a rational fashion. My father must have known that if he had tried the strawberry ice cream at the start, things wouldn't have degenerated to this point. But he hadn't, and now he was being paid back in kind, although it seemed like pure malevolence to him. I sensed that he was prepared to force the vendor to taste it. The vendor, on the other hand, was in what he thought was a win-win situation: he could try the ice cream and even if it turned out to have an odd, slightly bitter or medicinal taste, he could launch into an endless debate about the incommunicability or undecideability of taste sensations. At that moment two teenagers walked in. The ice cream vendor turned to them with a look of triumph on his face.

"Two one-peso cones."

The one-peso ice creams were big: four scoops. At the time two pesos was a considerable sum. The scene underwent a radical change. It was transformed by a new light, the light of prosperity and normality; the wide world had entered the shop in the form of those two teenagers. The sinister figure of the madman complaining about some nuance in the flavor of a ten-cent ice cream had been swept aside. This opening up of the situation called for new rules. Rational rules, which had been lacking. Any relationship, even (or especially) mine with Dad, has its rules. But there were also the general rules for the game of life.

The ice cream vendor was quick to realize this, and it was the last thing he realized. Without changing his triumphant expression, he said, "Let's see about this strawberry then."

He was talking more to the newcomers than to Dad. It was the clincher, his final show of mastery. My father was still holding the sad little cone of melted ice cream. The vendor wasn't going to taste that mess; he would sample his good ice cream, untouched and fresh from the drum.

Dad got worried. He felt defeated. "No, try this . . ." he said. But he said it without much conviction. It didn't make sense. And yet, in a way, it did. All things considered, he was right to keep that card up his sleeve. If the ice cream from the drum turned out to be all right, he could still fall back on the cone.

The vendor lifted the lid, took a clean spoon, scraped

the surface with it and lifted it to his mouth like a connoisseur. The reaction was instantaneous and automatic. He spat to one side. "You're right. It's horrible. I hadn't tried it."

He said it just like that. Like the most natural thing in the world. It didn't occur to him to say sorry. It really was out of order. It was too much for Dad. Hatred, the destructive instinct, overwhelmed him in an instant with the force of a physical blow.

"Is that all you've got to say to me? After . . ."

"Hey, calm down! How was I supposed to know?"

At this point, the only option left open, the only way forward, for both of them, was sheer, untrammeled violence. Neither was about to back down. Dad leant over the counter to thump the ice cream vendor, who braced himself behind the cash register. The two teenagers ran out, past me (I was standing on the threshold, transfixed, engaged in a warped attempt to connect up the different logics that had supplanted one another in the course of the dispute) and watched from outside. Dad had jumped over the counter and was aiming all his punches at his opponent's head. The vendor was fat, clumsy, and unable to hit back; all he could do was shield himself, more or less. Dad was shouting like a lunatic. He was beside himself. A punch that happened to land square on the vendor's ear spun him through ninety degrees. He ended up facing away from Dad, who grabbed him by the nape of the neck with both hands, pushed up against him from behind (as if he were raping him), and put his head into the drum of strawberry ice cream, which was still open.

"Go on, eat it! Eat it!"

"Nooo! Get him . . . uggh . . . off me!"

"Go on . . .!"

"Uggh!!"

"Eat it!"

With herculean force he shoved the vendor's face into the ice cream and kept pressing down. The victim's movements became spasmodic, less and less frequent . . . and eventually stopped altogether.

3

I NEVER KNEW HOW I got out of the ice-cream store
. . . or was taken away . . . or what happened . . . I lost consciousness, my body began to dissolve . . . literally . . . My
organs deliquesced . . . turning to green and blue bags of
slime hanging from stony necroses . . . with no life but the
cold fire of infection . . . and decomposition . . . swellings
. . . bundles of ganglia . . . A heart the size of a lentil, numb
with cold, beating in the midst of the ruins . . . a faltering
whistle in my twisted trachea . . . nothing more . . .

I was a victim of the terrible cyanide contamination . . .
the great wave of lethal food poisoning that was sweeping
Argentina and the neighboring countries that year . . .
The air was thick with fear, because it struck when least

expected; any foodstuff could be contaminated, even the most natural . . . potatoes, pumpkin, meat, rice, oranges . . . In my case it was ice cream. But even food lovingly prepared at home could be poisoned . . . Children were the most vulnerable . . . they had no resistance. Housewives were at their wit's end. A mother could kill her baby with baby food. It was a lottery . . . So many conflicting theories . . . So many deaths . . . The cemeteries were filling up with little tombstones, tenderly inscribed . . . Our angel has flown to the arms of the Lord . . . signed: his inconsolable parents. I got off lightly. I survived. I lived to tell the tale . . . but in the end I had to pay a high price . . . like they say: Buy cheaply, pay dearly.

My illness duplicated itself. I should have expected it . . . had I been capable of expecting anything, which I certainly wasn't. The affliction manifested itself as a kind of cruel equivalence. While my body writhed in physical pain, elsewhere, for different reasons, my soul was subjected to an equivalent torture. My soul . . . the fever . . . In those days it wasn't standard practice to control fever with medication . . . They let it run its course, interminably . . . I was in a state of unremitting delirium, with plenty of time to concoct the most baroque stories . . . I had my ups and downs, I suppose, but the stories followed one another in a sustained rush of invention . . . They fused into one, which was the reverse of a story . . . because my anxiety was the only story I had, and the fantasies didn't settle or hang together . . . So I couldn't even enter them and lose myself . . .

One of the forms the story took was the Flood. I was at home . . . back in Pringles, in the house we had left to come to Rosario . . . which was no longer ours . . . we would never live there again. The water was rising, and I was in bed, staring at the roof, rigid with fear . . . I couldn't even turn my head to see the water . . . but reflections from the rising surface were making whitish loops on the ceiling . . . It was pure fiction, with no basis in reality, because we had never even come close to being flooded . . .

Another form of the story: I was offering poisoned chocolates to my parents . . . Chocolate on the outside, then a very thin layer of glass, and, inside, a solution of arsenic in alcohol . . . There was no antidote . . . No way back . . . Dad took one, Mom too . . . I wanted to rewind time, I was sorry, but it was too late . . . They were going to die . . . The police would have no trouble establishing the cause of death . . . they would interrogate me . . . I decided to confess everything, to cry rivers of tears and let the current sweep me away . . . But even death was no consolation, since without Mom and Dad how could I live anyway? And the worst thing was that it was unheard of for a little girl to kill her parents . . . absolutely unheard of . . .

And another (but this was an alternative version of the Flood): an animal swimming in the inundated house, an otter . . . It would bite our feet if we tried to walk in the rising water . . . If my hand slipped from the sheet it would eat my fingers one by one . . .

Yet another: I was still rigid with fear, my head propped

up on a thick pillow, and my mother went to open the cupboard with green glass doors opposite the bed, in which I kept my books...To tell the truth I didn't have any books: I was too young, I hadn't learnt to read ... I began to panic ... I could hardly breathe ...What had Mom gone to get from the cupboard? Could she have known? She was taking advantage of my helplessness to ... Any moment now she would find it, my secret ... Stop, Mom! Don't do it! It will only bring you grief, the most terrible grief of your life! A grief to match my shame and terror ...

Needless to say there was no secret ... I never had any secrets, although, at the same time, everything was a secret, but not on purpose ... Delirium provided a model, and not just a model ... Mom was rummaging through the cupboard ... as the waters rose ... instead of doing something useful, like picking me up and carrying me in her arms across the fields, over the flooded plains to a safe place! I hated her for that ... She went on searching, in a daze, although the otter, who had suddenly become my accomplice, was gnawing at her ankles under the water ... and I knew that she had only minutes left to live, the poison would already be taking effect ... that is, if she had eaten the chocolate. And I hoped to God she had!

I hoped ... if only ... But no. It wasn't a matter of this or that happening ... but of how the events were combined, or rather the order in which they occurred ...The ordering was different ... They were repeating themselves

. . . Or rather, drifting free. . . When it was really bad, I wondered if I was going crazy.

Over all these stories hovered another, more conventional in a way, but more fantastic too. Separate from the series, it functioned like a "background," always there. It was a kind of static story . . . a chilling episode, with a wealth of horrific details . . . It filled me with dread, making the four-part delirium seem like light entertainment by comparison . . . Except that it wasn't just one more element, a bolt of lightning in a stormy sky . . . it was everything that was happening to me . . . everything that would happen to me in an eternity that had not yet begun and would never end . . . I was the girl in an illustrated book of fairy tales; I had become a myth . . . I was seeing it from inside . . .

From inside . . . I was alone in the house. Mom and Dad had gone to a wake and they had left me shut inside . . . in that little old house in Pringles where we no longer lived . . . alone with my four cartoon stories going round and round in my head . . . my crown of thorns . . . the two doors were locked, the wooden shutters closed . . . a safe for my parents' living treasure: me. The realism was meticulous, hermetic . . . But when I say that I was alone, that the house was locked, that it was night, these are not circumstances, or sundry elements that could be linked in a series . . . The series (the flood, the otter, the chocolates, the secret) was out there, using up all the delirium my fever could generate. . . The only thing left in here was reality, in one great cumbersome, wildly plausible block. . .

I had been sternly instructed not to open the door to anyone, under any circumstances. As if I needed to be told! My life depended on it, and not only my life. It was the first time I had been left on my own (this never happened in reality) but it was unavoidable . . . The first time is always frightening, because of the unknown . . . I was confident, the instructions were simple . . . Don't open the door. I could do that. It was easy. They could trust me. Anyway, who would come, at midnight . . .? My life and my safety depended on the answer to that question . . . Who, who, who could it be?

But someone was knocking at the front door! Beating as if they wanted to break it down! They weren't just knocking: they were trying to get in . . . Why would they want to do that, if not to kill me? And I was alone . . . ! They must have known . . . they knew perfectly well; that was why they had come . . . At best, they were burglars . . . The security of the house was in my hands, but my hands were so feeble. I was shaking like a leaf, on the other side of the door . . . Why had they left me on my own? What was so important that they had to abandon me?

The worst thing was . . . it was them . . . it was Mom and Dad knocking at the door! The monsters had taken on the appearance of my Mom and Dad . . . I don't know how I saw them, through the keyhole, I guess, standing on tip-toe . . . I got goose-pimples from head to foot, I froze . . .

the likeness was amazing . . . they had stolen their faces, their clothes, their hair . . . not much hair from Dad because he was bald, but all Mom's red curls . . . They were perfect imitations, flawless . . . The trouble they had gone to! Those beings who had no form, or wouldn't reveal it to me . . . those simulacra . . . with their sinister intentions . . . Terror froze my blood, I couldn't think . . .

They were thumping at the door in a frenzy; I don't know how it withstood the onslaught . . . They were shouting my name, they had been shouting for hours . . . with Mom and Dad's voices . . . Even the voices! But slightly different, slightly hoarse . . . They had drunk cognac at the wake, and they weren't used to it . . . they were going crazy . . . They had lost the key, or left it somewhere . . . some story . . . their lying was so transparent . . . They were insulting me! They were saying awful things! And I was crying, horrified, dumb, transfixed . . .

Dad jumped over the wall into the yard, he went to the kitchen door and started beating on it, kicking it . . . I walked through the darkened house, like a sleepwalker, stopped in front of the kitchen door and prayed to God it would hold . . . and my prayer was answered, for once . . . he went back to the front door. . .

Even if I'd wanted to let them in, how could I? I was locked in. I didn't have the key . . . Or did I?

That was beside the point. Did I want to let them in or not? Of course not. They hadn't fooled me . . . Or had they? How could I tell? They were exactly like my parents, more real than the real thing . . . I kept my eye to the keyhole, hypnotized by that unreal scene . . . But there they were in the midst of that unreality, my parents, it really was them . . . Not just their masks, but also their expressions, their tics, their style, their stories . . . That was how I saw my parents, especially Dad . . . it was different with Mom . . . I didn't see Dad's outward appearance as other people did . . . I saw the way he was, his past, his reactions, his reasoning . . . it was the same with Mom, now that I think of it . . . not that I was especially insightful, but they were my parents, so they had no form, or didn't reveal it to me . . . or wouldn't . . . that was the tragedy of my childhood and my whole life . . . My vision couldn't be satisfied with what was visible, it had to go rushing on, beyond, into the abyss, dragging me along behind . . .

The blows were deafening, the house was shaking on its foundations . . . the shouts grew louder . . . they were telling me in no uncertain terms . . . without words now . . . but I could understand anyway . . . But can't you see it's us? Can't you see it's us, you idiot? Idiot!

No! My parents wouldn't talk to me like that . . . they loved me, respected me . . . and yet . . . sometimes they lost their temper . . . I was a difficult girl, a problem child in a sense . . . and the assailants knew that, they were using it . . . all the world's evil was the clay from which they had molded those two ghastly dummies . . .

What would become of me? Would I fall into their hands? Would they get in? Would I open the door in a reckless moment, without thinking, prompted by an idiotic optimism . . . ? Would I believe them?

How could I tell? That was the worst thing: there was no end to it . . . Or rather: there was. Because if the only thing missing had been the end, in a way I could have stayed calm, waiting for it . . . putting it off, leaving it for later . . . But the waiting *was* the end! It was and it wasn't . . . It almost seemed like nothing at all. Because I couldn't see anything, the delirium wasn't strong enough, or it was too strong . . . I couldn't see the house in which I was trapped, I couldn't see the horrendous mannequins besieging it . . . the souls of Mom and Dad . . . It wasn't a hallucination . . . If only it had been: what a relief! No, it was a force . . . an invisible radiation . . .

It lasted a month. Amazingly, I survived. I could say: I woke up. Coming out of the delirium was like being released from prison. It would have been logical to feel relieved, but I didn't. Something had broken inside me, a valve, the little safety device that used to allow me to switch levels.

4

WHEN I REGAINED consciousness, I found myself in the pediatric ward of the Rosario Central Hospital.

I opened my eyes and found myself in a world that was new to me: the world of mothers. Dad didn't come to visit me once. But every single day I waited for him, with a mixture of longing and apprehension that prolonged my delirious trains of thought in a milder form. Mom came, though, and the scent of terror she brought with her was like Dad's shadow. There was no escaping it, because now I was locked into the system of accumulation, in which nothing is ever left behind. I didn't ask her about him. She was different. She seemed distracted, worried, anxious. She didn't stay long; she said she had things to do, and I understood. The other beds were attended twenty-four hours a day by mothers, aunts and grandmothers taking turns. I was alone, a daughter abandoned in a maternal realm.

There were about forty children in the ward with me, with all sorts of conditions, from broken bones to leukemia. I never counted them, or made any friends; I didn't even speak to any of them.

It took them forever to discharge me, so all the beds were vacated and reoccupied during my stay, ten times or more in some cases. There were all sorts, from kids who seemed to be in excellent health and made a phenomenal racket, to others who were listless, lying still or asleep . . . I was in the second category. I was so weak I couldn't move, and permanently drowsy. A kind of lethargy would set in mid-afternoon and last for hours. I didn't even swivel my eyes. Sometimes it went on for whole days or weeks; I could feel myself falling back into that state without having come out of it, at least not consciously . . . And it was a very long way to fall . . .

Every day, just at the worst time, or the beginning of the worst time, the doctor came to visit me. He must have been interested in my case; survivors of the cyanide poisoning were rare. I once heard him pronounce the word "miracle." If there had been a miracle, it was entirely involuntary. I was not cooperating with science. An urge, a whim or a manic obsession that not even I could explain impelled me to sabotage the doctor's work, to trick him. I pretended to be stupid . . . I must have thought the opportunity was too good to waste. I could be as stupid as I liked, with impunity. But it wasn't simply a matter of passive resistance. Doing nothing at all was too haphazard, because sometimes nothing can be the right response, and I was determined not to let chance determine my fate. So even though I could have left his questions unanswered, I took the trouble to answer them. I lied. I said the opposite of the truth, or the opposite of what seemed truest to me. But again it wasn't simply a matter of saying the opposite . . . He soon learned how to formulate his questions so that the answer was a simple yes or no. If I had *always* lied, he would have started translating every answer into its opposite. I considered it my duty to lie every time; so in order to protect myself, I had to proceed in a roundabout way, which isn't all that easy when you have to reply yes or no, without hedging. On top of this, I had resolved never to mix any truth with my lies. I was afraid that if I lost track, chance would be able to intervene. I don't know how I did it, but I managed somehow. Here are some of my tricks (I don't know why I'm explaining all this, unless I'm hoping to inspire other patients by my example): I pretended not to have heard a question, and when he asked another, I replied to the first one, with a lie, of course; I replied, always fallaciously, to one element of the question, for example an adjective or a verb tense, not to the question as a whole; he would ask me "Is this where it was hurting?" and I would answer "No," while suggesting with an ingenious movement of my eyebrows that the place in question was not where it *was* hurting before, but where it was hurting now. He picked up all these signals—nothing was lost on him—and despondently rephrased his question: "Is this where it's hurting?" But by then I had already moved on to a new system, a new tactic . . . I should say in my defense that I was making it all up as I went along. Although I had veritable eons of time in which to think, I never used that time to plan my lies.

"And how are we today, young Master César? Don't we look well? Ready to play ball again? Let's see how we're going . . ."

His cheerfulness was contagious. He was a short young man with a little moustache. He seemed to come from far away.

From the outside world. I looked at him with a special face I had invented, which meant, What? What? What are you talking about? Why are you asking all these hard questions? Can't you see the state I'm in? Why are you talking to me in Chinese instead of Spanish? He lowered his eyes, but took it as well as he could. He sat on the edge of the bed and began to examine me. He poked me with his finger here and there, in the liver, the pancreas, the gall bladder . . .

"Does it hurt here?"

"Yes."

"Does it hurt here?"

"No."

"Here?"

"Yes."
"Yes?"
" . . . "

Then, perplexed, he started all over again. He was looking for places where it had to be hurting, where an absence of pain was impossible. But he couldn't find them; I was the sole keeper and mistress of the impossible. I possessed the keys to pain . . .

"Does it hurt a little bit here?"

I made it clear that his questions had tired me out. I burst into tears and he tried to comfort me.

He used his stethoscope. I believed that I could accelerate my heartbeat at will, and maybe I could. At once he began to manipulate me with extreme care. For some reason he wanted to put the stethoscope on my back, so he had to sit me up, which turned out to be as difficult as standing a broom handle on end. When he finally succeeded, I began rolling my head around wildly and retching. Fiction and reality were fused at this point; my simulation was becoming real, tinting all my lies with truth. For me, retching was something sacred, something not to be trifled with. The memory of Dad in the ice-cream store made retching more real than reality itself; it was the thing that made everything else real, and nothing could withstand it. For me, ever since, it has been the essence of the sacred, the source from which my calling sprang.

When the doctor moved on, I was a complete wreck. I could hear him at the beds nearby, talking and laughing; I could hear the voices of the little patients answering his questions . . . All this came to me through a thick fog. I could feel myself plummeting into the abyss . . . My willfulness wasn't deliberate. It was just plain willfulness, of the most primitive kind; it had taken control of me, as evolution takes control of a species. I had succumbed to it during my sickness or perhaps just before its onset; I wasn't like that normally. On the contrary, if I had one salient character trait, it was willingness to cooperate. That man, the doctor, was a kind of hypnotist who had put a spell on me. The worst thing was that, even under his spell, I was perfectly consciousness of being willful.

Mom didn't miss a single one of the doctor's visits . . . She hovered at a discreet distance and came forward to help as soon as I became unmanageable . . . She was extremely anxious to extract information from him. He used the word "shock" . . . He can't have been a real intellectual, because he showed great interest in what Mom said to him. They went away and whispered; I had no idea what about . . . I didn't know that we had been in the papers. He said "shock" again, and repeated it over and over . . .

But the doctor and Mom were hardly more than a brief distraction in the course of the day, which stretched before me, majestically impassive, rolling out from morning to night. It didn't seem long, but it filled me with a kind of respect. Each instant was different and new and unrepeatable. That was the very nature of time, ceaselessly realizing itself, in every life . . . My malicious little strategies seemed so petty, I was overcome with shame . . .

Ana Módena de Collon-Michet, the nurse, was the day incarnate. There was only one nurse in the ward through-out the day shift; just one nurse for forty little patients . . . It might seem insufficient and no doubt it was. Resources were rather stretched at the Rosario Central Hospital. But no one complained. All the patients were hoping to get out of there alive, one way or another, all fondly imagining that they would not be back. Even the children were fooling themselves, quite unwittingly.

But the days came to rest in the big white ward and wherever I turned my gaze, there was the nurse. Ana Módena was a living hieroglyph. She never left the hospi-tal; she had no illusions. She was a ghost.

The mothers were always complaining about her; they fought with her, but they must have known it was hope-less. The mothers came and went, while she remained. Short-lived alliances were forged against her, and Mom was involved on a number of occasions; she didn't have the strength of character to say no, even when she realized it would have been in her best interests. The complaints con-cerned Ana Módena's abruptness, her impatience, her rudeness, her almost insane ignorance. Having frequented the hospital environment for an average of a week, the mothers formed an idea of the ideal nurse for the children's ward. They imagined what she would be like, what each of

them would have been like in her place: a good fairy, all
gentleness and understanding . . . It wasn't hard; without
realizing, they were imagining how the ideal nurse would
have been gentle and understanding with *them*, and each of
us is the ultimate expert on the gentleness and understanding we deserve. It wasn't their fault; they were poor,
ignorant women, housewives struggling to cope. In nine
cases out of ten, they were responsible for the illnesses of
their children . . . They had a right to dream . . . They
thought they knew what the perfect nurse would be like,
and they did . . . Their mistake was to go one step further
and presume that all those qualities could be combined in
a single woman . . . The fact that Ana Módena, the Perón
of the Pediatric Ward, was exactly the opposite of their
ideal image, cast them into a stupor which they could only
shake off, or so they felt, by drawing up a list of demands
or devising a strategy with the aim of having her dismissed
. . . All those dreams turned her into a ghost. As a rule I did-
n't understand what was going on, but this was something
I understood, because I was a dreamer . . . and because Ana
Módena was a ghost in other ways too. She was always in
a rush, extremely busy, as any nurse would have been in
that situation, looking after a forty-bed ward on her own.
But she was never available for anyone. She was invariably
busy with the others, and it was the same for all of them
too. As I lay there, I got used to seeing her out of the corner of my eye, whizzing past from dawn to dusk . . . never
stopping . . . It wasn't only the children in their beds that

she had to attend to, but also those being sent off to the operating theatre, or for X-rays . . . and she did it all so badly, whispered the mothers, that everything kept going wrong because of her . . . They said she kept losing patients . . . They keep dying . . . as if her touch was lethal . . . They're always dying in her ward, said the legend that enveloped me like a bandage made of whispering phylacteries . . . The children stopped living when they fell into the category of things she was simply too busy to deal with . . . But this wretched reputation didn't prevent the mothers from making up to her, flattering her, leaving her tips, bringing her little cakes and being unbelievably, shockingly servile . . . After all, the greatest treasures they possessed, their children, were in her hands.

She was a fat, hefty woman. When she bore down on me, it was like an elephant splashing in a puddle . . . I was the water. There was something sublime about her clumsiness . . . She suffered from a peculiar affliction: for her, left was right and vice versa. Down was up, forward was back . . . The meager volume of my body came apart in her hands . . . legs, arms, head . . . each extremity was subjected to a different gravitational force . . . I was breaking up into falls and imbalances . . . With her, there was no point pretending . . . she projected me into another dimension . . . yet various parts of my body, suddenly scattered far and wide, took it on themselves to pretend . . . though what, I don't know . . . Her hands, with their lethal touch, were molding an absolute truth.

They kept me alive with serum. Ana Módena replaced the bottles, invariably at the wrong time, and put the needles in my arm . . . She stuck them in anywhere. My nose began to run. Everything that went in my arm came out of my nose, in a continuous drip. It was an extremely rare case. To her, it seemed normal . . . In any case it wasn't a priority. Early in the morning, before the first mother arrived, Ana Módena brought the dwarf, and made her recite her psalms in front of each bed, including the empty ones. The dwarf was an autistic visionary. Ana Módena steered her by the shoulders, as if she were holding the handlebars of a tricycle. The dwarf didn't seem to see anything; she was a piece of furniture . . . She was one of those dwarves with an oversize head . . . Ana Módena would put her in front of a bed occupied by a listless or sleeping child . . . a deep silence reigned in the ward . . . Then, responding to a tap between the shoulder blades, the dwarf would mutter a Hail Mary, gesticulating oddly with her little arms . . .

"Mother Corita will save you, not the doctors!" thundered Ana Módena.

The dwarf passed like a comet . . . Everything happened automatically . . . It was a blanket cure: empty and occupied beds received the same blessing . . . Thus religion was smuggled into the world of sickness. Except that it was an open secret, and, of all that brute's misdeeds, this was the one the mothers brought up first if they had any pretensions to scientific decorum . . . but as soon as a doctor seemed unsure, or a child fell ill again or began to vomit, it was: Bring the dwarf, I beg you . . . Bring her to save my little angel . . . The hypocrites! Severely, Ana Módena would reply: It is the Virgin who saves, not the dwarf . . . And the mothers: For mercy's sake, bring the little dwarf . . .

Mother Corita was the hospital's real cement; Ana Módena was just its representative. The dwarf stopped the hospital exploding into a thousand pieces . . . and my body with it . . . my head flying off to the north, my legs to the south, an arm here, a finger there . . . Believing in the dwarf was what made it all hang together . . . the life fluid flowed through her, through the tube, from my arm up to my nose . . . But I had to believe. I had to believe deep down, while pretending not to.

Then it occurred to me that . . . with my body coming apart . . . I might reach a point at which I could no longer believe in the dwarf. Me, of all people! The perfect hypnotic subject! I believed in everything! And I needed my belief to remain intact!

But what if the dwarf was a fake? What if I *couldn't* believe in her? After all, was I so different? Wasn't I unbelievable myself, objectively? So what was to stop her being like me? Or, worse still, what was to stop me being a sort of dwarf, an emanation of Mother Corita . . .?

I needed a confirmation. I tried to extract one from Ana Módena . . . I tried to get to the bottom of things. And so it was that one morning, when she came into range, I blurted, "I dreamt about a dwarf."

"What?"

"I dreamt about a dwarf."

"What? What dwarf?"

I had thrown her.

"I dreamt about a dwarf who had a thorn stuck in her heart."

"*What* dwarf?"

"A dwarf . . . a doowarf . . . a doo waruff . . ."

There could be no doubt about the identity of the dwarf . . . The aim of my ruse was to make her think I had something "difficult" to express. I had to approach it indirectly, resorting to allegory or fiction pure and simple. And she was drawn in, obliged to engage with my clever ploys . . . which escaped her . . . And then I began to lie by telling the truth (and vice versa) though how, I don't know . . . it escaped me too . . . My strategies died, like the children in the ward . . . and came back to life with a vengeance . . . In a desperate bid to communicate concepts refractory to the understanding of a little girl completely stupefied by her wretched physical state, Ana Módena began to use gestures . . . Gestures took over . . . She was an impulsive, unmethodical woman and fell into the trap of trusting intuition, which flies blind and reaches the target before understanding can set to work . . . Hastiness and clumsiness made all her movements blunder into one another . . . As for me, the dismemberment made me gesticulate like her mirror image . . . but it was dizzying, the meanings of her grimaces and looks and intonations were piling up absurdly . . . the accumulation seemed to be approaching a limit, a threshold . . . coming closer and closer . . .

And at that point something snapped. I don't think it was something in me so much as something between the two of us. But no: it *was* in me, inside me. From that moment on I have suffered from a peculiar perceptive dysfunction: I can't understand mime; I'm deaf (or blind, I'm not sure how to put it) to the language of gestures. I have on occasion, in subsequent years, attended mime shows . . . and while the four-year old children around me understood perfectly what was being represented, and screamed with laughter, all I could see were pointless movements, an abstract gesticulation . . . It's funny, now that I think of it, that no mime artist, not even the best, not even Marcel Marceau himself (who is the hardest of all to understand for me), has ever tried to mime a dwarf . . . Why should that be? In the language of gestures, the dwarf must be the unsayable.

5

BECAUSE OF MY ILLNESS, I started school three months late, in June. I still can't understand why they accepted me at that stage in the year and put me in with the children who had started on time. Especially since it was first grade, the absolute beginning of my school life (there was no such thing as kindergarten back then), such a crucial and delicate stage. It's even harder to understand why Mom insisted on getting me in, why she went to the trouble of making them take me; it can't have been easy. She must have begged, implored them, got down on her knees. I can imagine it; that was her idea of motherhood. She probably thought she wouldn't know what to do with me at home for another whole year. But what with the work of taking me to school, going to fetch me afterwards, washing and ironing the smocks, buying the pencils, pens, rulers and so on, finding an old reader to borrow, in the end it must have seemed hardly worth it, just for the relief of having me off her hands for a few hours a day at siesta time. She probably thought she was doing it for my good. It didn't occur to her that missing three months, the *first* three months, in first grade, would be too much even for a girl like me. But it wouldn't be fair to blame her. I don't. It was only three months, after all. And poor Mom had so many things on her mind at the time. All the same, the teacher and the principal should have known better. But perhaps they were too close to the problems of learning, just as Mom was too far away from them.

The first weeks were a stream of pure images. Human beings tend to make sense of experience by imbuing it with continuity: what is happening now can be explained by what happened before. So it's not surprising that I persisted in the perceptual habits I had recently acquired with Ana Módena and went on seeing gestures, mimicry, stories without sound, in which I had no part. No one had explained the purpose of school to me, and I wasn't about to work it out for myself. Initially, however, the problem didn't seem serious. I regarded it all, rather stubbornly, as a spectacle, an acrobatic show . . .

The drama started later on . . . Why is it that drama always starts late? Whereas comedy always seems to have started already. Except that later on we come to see that it was the other way around . . . The drama was triggered for me by the realization that the mute scene I was witnessing, the teacher's and pupils' abstract mimicry, affected me vitally. It was *my* story, not someone else's. The drama had begun as soon as I had set foot in the school, and it was unfolding before me, entire and timeless. I was and was not involved in it; I was present, but not a participant, or participating only by my refusal, like a gap in the performance, but that gap was me! At least I had finally realized (and for this I should have been grateful) why I was missing out on the mental soundtrack: I couldn't read. My little classmates could. By some sort of miracle, they had learned how to in those first three months; an abyss had opened between them and me. An inexplicable abyss, a void, precisely because there was no way to account for the leap. They couldn't say how or exactly when they had learned to read, nor could I, of course; not even the teacher could have explained it. It was simply something that had happened. For the teacher (who had forty years of experience with the first grade) it was routine: it happened every year. It was so familiar, it had become invisible, a blind spot.

The curtain went up for me one day, in the boy's bathroom at school . . . But first I need to explain the circumstances, otherwise the anecdote will be incomprehensible.

We lived on the outskirts of Rosario, in a modest neighborhood, and most of the children at the local school came from humble families, often living just above the poverty line, or below it. At the time, children from what

would now be called "marginal" families all went to
school, at least for a few years. There were no special
schools or educational psychologists . . . It was a very
rough, very wild environment, a Darwinian struggle for
life. The fights were bloody, and the vocabulary that
accompanied them was brutal. I knew about swear words;
I even knew the words themselves, but for some reason I
had never paid them much attention. It was as if I regis-
tered them with a second sense of hearing and transferred
them to another level of perception. I had come to the
conclusion that they functioned as a set and their meaning
was a kind of action, which wasn't too far from the truth.
There was only one element that stood out from the set.
Usually, when the boys at school were arguing, the transi-
tion from verbal to physical abuse was signaled by one of
them suddenly saying, in the midst of what was, for me, a
nebulous mass of swear words, "He insulted my mother."

I didn't find this detail bewildering in itself, because the
mother figure was sacred for me too, and I had noticed that
"mother" was often included in the flow of swear words.
Had I been asked, I think I could have even repeated the
whole sentence, having heard it so often: "Your mother's a
bitch." Now, except for that central word, the rest was
meaningless noise to me. I was almost unimaginably vague,
not because I was stupid, but because nothing really mattered to me. This is an enormous paradox, because everything mattered to me, far too much; I made a mountain out
of every molehill, and that was my main problem . . . I

might have seemed indifferent, but nothing could have been further from the truth and I knew it. This incident was a case in point. I must have noticed that sometimes a kid would say "He insulted my mother" without the word "mother" having been pronounced, but I let it pass, and thinking back over the whole incident, I concluded, for my own convenience, that "mother" must have been said, I must have missed it. On one occasion, however, I was forced to abandon this explanation. There was a fight at playtime, near the windmill at the back of the schoolyard. Whenever there was a fight, everyone went to see, gathering round in a circle two or three deep; there was no way it could go unnoticed. Then one of the teachers would come to break up the feral boxing match. But plunging into those mêlées was not for the faint-hearted, and only a small group of "tough" teachers dared to intervene, one especially, a strapping young lady, and she was the one who came this time. The contenders were two boys from the third grade, covered in blood, their smocks torn, both of them in a mad frenzy. The teacher pried them apart, not without difficulty. The bigger of the two went back to his gang of friends. The other one began to bawl. He was hic-coughing through his tears . . . one of my specialties. The teacher demanded an explanation at the top of her voice but he couldn't speak. It was as if the fight was still going on in his heart. He looked so wretched, the teacher took him in her arms and hugged him tight. She guessed the explanation, which he finally managed to utter between violent sobs, "He insulted my mother." She calmed him, hugged him . . . As a tough teacher she could understand; they lived in the same world, after all. The other boy was watching from a distance, surrounded by his friends, fury and resentment flaring in his eyes . . . Meanwhile, for the first time, I felt a note of boundless bewilderment resonating: Mother? What mother? What was he talking about? Why did everyone seem to accept what he said?

I had witnessed the brawl from the very start, I was certain I hadn't missed anything and I knew that at no point had the word "mother" been pronounced. The other words, yes, but not that one. It was so clear, I could only conclude that "mother" must have been *implied* somehow. And of all the things I might have fastened on, that was what intrigued me most of all; I couldn't get it out of my head.

Anyway, one day, in the middle of a lesson, I asked the teacher for permission to go to the bathroom. I was always doing this; we all were. I asked without needing to go or having carefully chosen my moment (I guess it was the same for the others). I did it on impulse. It's the only unalloyed triumph I can remember from my childhood. As soon as the teacher saw the little hand go up, she would briefly consider what the pupil was going to miss (it was always something trivial like when to write b and when to write v) and then shout: All right! But this is the last time! The *last* time! And the kid who had been visited by the brilliant idea of asking at precisely that moment, which had turned out to be the last, ran out of the classroom, deliriously happy, under the hateful, bitter gaze of all the others, who felt they had missed their last chance . . . But the chance was repeated, identically, and seized, four or five times in every one-hour period. For us it was always now or never and the teacher always repeated her ultimatum, although she never said no, because the first-grade teachers, who were immune to other kinds of anxiety, lived in fear of the kids wetting themselves. But we didn't know that. We were just kids. The amazing thing is that I managed to join in the game. It would have been much more like me to hold on until my bladder burst. But no. I asked without needing to go, like all the others. I wasn't backward in that respect, at least.

My anomalous behavior can perhaps be explained by a magically repeated coincidence. Every time I asked for permission to go to the bathroom, two or three times a day and always on the spur of the moment, as I was crossing the deserted yard, I met a boy heading in the same direction, a boy from another grade, I don't know which. We ended up becoming friends. His name was Farías. Or was it Quiroga? Now that I'm trying to remember, I'm getting the names mixed up. Or maybe there were two of them.

This time, he was there, as usual, although we had never dreamed of arranging to meet. The dark grey walls of the bathroom were covered with graffiti. The kids were always stealing chalk so they could write on them. I had never really paid much attention to the inscriptions.

Farías pointed one out to me; it was large and recent. After a few days of exposure to the powerful ammoniac fumes of the bathroom the chalk began to darken. These letters were so white they shone—so they must have been fresh that day. They were capital letters, fiercely legible, though not for me; all I could see were horizontal and vertical sticks in a senseless tangle. Until that moment I had thought that the graffiti in the bathroom were drawings, incomprehensible drawings, runes or hieroglyphs. Farías waited for me to "read" the inscription, then he laughed. I laughed with him, in all sincerity. What a funny drawing! I really did find it amusing. What an idea! I thought. Incomprehensible drawings! But something prevented me from expressing this thought; my hypocrisy had recesses that were obscure even to me. Farías, however, spoke his mind; he made some smug and insinuating remark . . . I can't remember what. It was something about a mother. That was all it took, unfortunately. I understood, and it felt as if the world was crashing down on me.

I understood what it meant to read. Mothers were mixed up with that too! What I had mistaken for drawings, or some kind of recondite algebra in which the teachers specialized for reasons that were none of my concern, turned out to mean the things that people said, things that could be said anywhere, by anyone, even me. I thought it was just school stuff, but it was the stuff of life itself. Words, silent words, mimicry, the process by which words signified themselves . . . I understood that *I didn't know how to read,* and the others did. That's what it had all been about, all that I had suffered in ignorance. In an instant I grasped the enormity of the disaster. Not that I was particularly intelligent or lucid; the understanding happened in me, but I had almost no part in it, and that was the most horrible thing. I stood there transfixed, staring at the inscription, as if it had hypnotized me. I don't know what I thought or decided to do . . . maybe nothing. The next thing I remember is sitting at my desk, where I vegetated day after day. I opened my virgin exercise book, picked up my pencil, which I still hadn't used, and reproduced that inscription from memory, stroke by stroke, without a single error or any idea what I was writing:

YOFUCKNSONFABITCHPUSSY

I should say that Farías had not read it out aloud, so I didn't know how those drawings translated into sound. And yet, as I wrote, *I knew.* Because knowledge is never monolithic. We know things in part. For example, I knew that they were swear words, that it was a conglomerate, that the mother was implied at some level; I knew about the violence, the fights, insulting the mother, the fury, the blood, the tears . . . There were other things I didn't know, but they were so inextricably entwined with the things I did know that I wouldn't have been able to tell them apart. As it happens, in this case there were things I wouldn't discover until much later on. Until the age of fourteen, I thought children came out of their mothers' belly buttons. And I discovered my mistake, at the age of fourteen, in a most peculiar way. I was reading an article about sex education in an issue of *Selecciones*, and in a paragraph about the ignorance in which young girls were kept in Japan, I found this scandalous example: a fourteen-year old Japanese girl had professed her belief that children came out of their mothers' belly buttons. That was exactly what I, a fourteen-year old Argentinean girl, believed. Except that from then on, I knew it wasn't true. And, rightly or wrongly, I pitied my Japanese counterpart.

That day back in first grade, when I went home, I couldn't wait for Mom to see what I had written. But the reason I couldn't wait was that I was terrified. I knew that something terrible would happen, but I didn't know what. I didn't take the exercise book out of my school bag; I didn't show it to Mom. She got it out herself and looked at it. Why? After the repeated disappointment of finding it blank, she had given up checking regularly and hadn't touched it for weeks. I must have given her some kind of signal. When she read it, she screamed and went pale. She was indignant for the rest of the day; she went on and on about it. That inscription was just what she had been waiting for; it unleashed her characteristic fighting spirit, which recent events had kept in check. It was an outlet for her. The next day she came to school with me and had an hour-long meeting with my teacher in the office. They called me in, but naturally they couldn't get a word out of me. Not that they needed to. From the veranda where I was waiting (the secretary had been sent to take care of the class for the duration of the meeting) I could hear Mom shouting, hurling abuse at the teacher, arguing relentlessly (always coming back to the fact that I didn't know how to read). It was a memorable day in the annals of Rosario's School Number 22. Finally, just before the bell rang, the teacher came out of the office, walked along the veranda and through the first door, into the classroom. As she went past, she neither looked at me nor invited me to follow; in fact, she didn't speak to me or look at me again for the rest of the year. Mom left during recess, but what with the chaos of kids and teachers, I didn't see her go. When the bell rang again, I went into the classroom as usual and sat down in my place. The teacher had recovered a bit, but not much. Her eyes were red; she looked terrible. For once, a dead silence reigned. Thirty pairs of childish eyes were fixed on her. She was standing in front of the blackboard. She tried to talk, but all that came out was a hoarse squawk. She stifled a sob. Moving stiffly, like a tailor's dummy, she stepped forward and tousled the hair of a boy sitting in the front row. The gesture was meant to be tender, and I'm sure that's how she felt, perhaps her heart had never been so full of tenderness, but her movements were so rigid that the boy cringed. She didn't notice and tousled his louse-ridden mop all the same. Then she did it to a second boy, and a third. She took a deep breath, and finally spoke:

"I always tell the truth. I stell it trueways. I children. I am the truth and the life. I trife. Strue. Childern. I am the second mother. Thecken smother. I love you all equally. I equal all of you for mother. I tell you the truth for love. The looth for trove. Momother love mother! For all of you! All of you! But there is one . . . bun their is wut . . . air ee wah . . ."

Her voice had gone all shrill and scratchy. She raised a vertical index finger. This was her only gesture during that memorable speech . . . The finger was steady but the rest of her was shaking; then, and simultaneously, the finger was shaking and the rest of her was steady as a block of metal . . . Tears ran down her cheeks. After this pause she went on:

"That Aira boy . . . He's here among you, and he doesn't seem any different. Maybe you haven't noticed him, he's so insignificant. But he's here. Don't be fooled. I always tell you the true, the theck, the trove. You are good, clever, sweet children. Even the ones who are naughty, or have to repeat, or get into fights all the time. You're normal, you're all the same, because you have a second mother. Aira is a moron. He might seem the same as you, but he's a moron all the same. He's a monster. He doesn't have a second mother. He's wicked. He wants to see me dead. He wants to kill me. But he's not going to succeed! Because you are going to protect me. You will protect me from the monster, won't you? Say it . . ."

" . . ."

"Say, 'Yes, Miss.'"

"Yes, Miss!"

"Louder!"

"Yeess Miiisss!"

"Say, Yis Mess Rodríguez."

"Yis Mess Ridróguez."

"Louder!"

"Yossmessriidroogueez!"

"Loouuder!!"

"Yiiissmooossreeedroooguiiiz!!"

"Good! Gggooood! Protect your teacher. She has forty years of experience. She could die any moment, and then it'll be too late to be sorry. The killer is after her. But it doesn't matter. I'm not saying all this for my sake, no, I've had my life already. Forty years teaching first grade. The first of the second mothers. I'm saying it for you. Because he wants to kill you too. Not me. You. But don't be afraid, teacher will protect you. You have to watch out for vipers, tarantulas and rabid dogs. And especially for Aira. Aira is a thousand times worse. Watch out for Aira! Don't go near him! Don't talk to him! Don't look at him! Pretend he doesn't exist. I always thought he was a moron, but I had nnno idea . . . I dddidn't realize . . . Now I do! Don't let him dirty you! Don't let him infect you! Don't even give him the time of day! Don't breathe when he's near. Die of asphyxiation if you have to, just so long as you freeze him out. He's a monster, a killer! And your mothers will cry if you die. They'll try and blame me, I know them. But if you watch out for the monster nothing will happen. Pretend he doesn't exist, pretend he's not there. If you don't talk to him or look at him, he can't harm you. Teacher will protect you. She is the second mother. Teacher loves you. I am the teacher. I always tell the truth . . ."

And so on, for quite a long time. At some point she started repeating herself, word for word, like a tape recorder. I was looking through her. I was looking at the blackboard where she had written: zebra, zero, zigzag . . . in perfectly formed letters . . . That calligraphy was her prettiest feature. And she had reached the letter Z . . . She seemed upset, but I didn't think she was talking nonsense. Everything was so real, it seemed transparent, and I was reading the words on the blackboard . . . I was reading . . . Because that day I had learned to read.

6

MEANWHILE, DAD WAS in prison for the business with the ice-cream vendor. One afternoon, Mom took me to visit him. It was logical, because I had been at the center, at the heart of the misadventure. Did they blame me? Yes and no. They couldn't really blame me—it would have been grossly unfair—but at the same time, they couldn't help blaming me, because I was the origin of it all. It was the same for me; I couldn't blame them for having these feelings, and yet I did. In any case, one or both of them had decided that it would be a good thing to take me along at visiting time. To show how his wife and daughter were standing by him and all that. How naïve. The Rosario remand center was a long way from home, right across town. We took a bus. Halfway there I had a panic attack for no reason and burst into tears. Up went the curtain of my private theater. Mom looked at me, unamazed. Yes, *una*-mazed.

"Are you going to tell me what's got into you?"

I didn't have anything very definite to say, but what came out took her completely by surprise, and me too.

"Where's my dad?"

The voice I put on! It was a squawk, but crystal clear, without the slightest stammer.

Mom glanced around. The bus was packed full and the people surrounding us, hearing my cry, had turned to look. She didn't know what to say.

"Where's my dad?" I raised my voice.

Poor Mom. Who could blame her for thinking I was doing it on purpose?

"You're going to see him soon," she said, without committing herself. She tried to change the subject, to distract me: "Look at the pretty flowers."

We were passing a house with superb flowerbeds in the front garden.

"Is he dead?"

There was no stopping me now. The other passengers were already intrigued by the story, and that excited me inordinately. Because I was the owner of the story. Mom put her arms around my shoulders and pulled me close.

"No, no. I already told you," she whispered, lowering her voice until it was almost inaudible.

"What?" I yelled.

"Shhh . . ."

"I can't hear you, Mom!" I shouted, shaking my head, as if I was afraid that the uncertainty about my dad would make me deaf.

She had no choice but to speak up. "You're going to see him soon."

"Yes, I'm going to see him. But is he dead?"

"No, he's alive."

I could sense the passengers' interest. The cityscape slid over the glass of the windows like a forgotten backdrop.

"Mom, where's Dad? Why doesn't he come home?"

I adopted a tone of voice that signified: "Stop lying to me. Let's behave like adults. I might look like I'm three years old, but I'm six, and I have a right to know the truth."

Mom had told me the whole truth. I knew he was in prison, waiting for the verdict: an eight-year sentence for homicide. I knew all that. The only reason for these untimely doubts of mine was to make her tell the story for the benefit of perfect strangers. How could her daughter be capable of such an idiotic betrayal? She couldn't believe it (nor could I). But the panic that I was exhibiting was all too real. As usual, I had managed to confuse her. It was easy: all I had to do was confuse myself.

"He's sick," she said in another inaudible whisper. "That's why we're going to visit him."

"Sick? Is he going to die? Like grandma?"

One of my grandmothers had died before I was born.

The other was in good health, in Pringles. We never used the expression "grandma" at home. That was a detail I added to make the scene more convincing.

"No. He's going to get better. Like you. You were sick and you got better, didn't you?"

"Did the ice cream make him sick?"

And so I went on until we arrived: Mom trying to shut me up all the way and me raising my voice, creating a real scene. When we got off the bus, she didn't say anything or ask me for an explanation. I felt that my performance had come to an end, a bad end, and that she was ashamed of me . . . The anxiety intensified and I began to cry again, with much more determination than before. The logical thing to do would have been to stop in the square, sit down on a bench and wait until I got over it. But Mom was tired, sick and tired of me and my carrying-on, and she headed straight for the prison. My tears dried up. I didn't want Dad to see me crying.

It was visiting time, of course. We joined the line; a lady who seemed nice enough frisked us, checked the string bag full of food that Mom had brought, and let us through. We were already in the visitors' yard. We had to wait a while for Dad. Mom was off in a world of her own (she didn't talk to the other women), so I got a chance to go exploring.

There were entries and exits all around the yard. It didn't seem to be hermetically sealed, which came as something of a surprise. It's hard not to have a romantic idea of what a prison will be like, even if you don't know what romanticism is (I certainly didn't). To tell the truth, I didn't know what a prison was either. This one was steeped in an intense, destructive realism, strong enough to dissolve all preconceived ideas, whether you had any or not.

I headed for a door, drawn as if by a magnet. Subliminally, I had noticed that there were other children in the yard, all holding their mothers' hands. A strong autumn sun bleached the surfaces. It was a sleepy time of day. I felt invisible.

Of all the places I knew, the one most like this prison was the hospital. People were shut in both places for a long time. But there was a difference. The reason you couldn't get out of the hospital was internal: the patient, as my own case had shown, was incapable of moving. There was some other reason why you couldn't get out of prison. I wasn't sure what it was: force was still a vague concept for me. I blended the ideas of prison and hospital. There was an invisible exchange between the two. Sickness could disappear and sick thought be transferred to others . . . It was the perfect escape plan . . . Perhaps Dad could come back home with us. In that excessively realist building, I was radiating magic . . . Since it was my fault that Dad was there . . .

But my magic started acting on me: a melancholy fantasy suddenly transported my soul to a region far, far away. Why didn't I have any dolls? Why was I the only girl in the world who didn't have a single doll? My dad was in prison . . . and I didn't have a doll to keep me company. I had never had one, and I didn't know why. It wasn't because my parents were poor or stingy (when did that ever stop a child?). There was some other mysterious reason . . . And yet, although the mystery remained, poverty was a factor. Especially now. Now we were going to be really poor, Mom and I: abandoned, all on our own. And that was why I felt the need of a doll so sharply, so painfully. True to my dramatic style, I surrendered to a nostalgic lament, rich in variations. The doll had disappeared forever, before I learnt the words with which to ask for it, leaving a gaping hole in the middle of my sentences . . . I saw myself as a lost doll, discarded, without a girl . . .

That was me. The inexistent girl. Living, I was dead. If I had died, Dad would have been free. The judges would have been merciful to the father who had taken a life for a life, especially since one was the life of his darling daughter and the other the life of a complete stranger. But I had survived. I wasn't the same as before, I could tell. I didn't know how or why, but I wasn't the same. For one thing, my memory had gone blank. I couldn't remember anything before the incident in the ice-cream store. Maybe I didn't even remember that properly. Maybe, in fact, the ice-cream vendor's life had been swapped for mine. I had begun to live when he died. That's why I felt like I was dead, dead and invisible . . .

When I reached the end of this train of thought, I found myself in a new place. I was inside. How had I got there? Where was Dad? This last question was the one that woke me up. It woke me up because it was so much like my dreams. I was alone, abandoned, invisible.

Either I had climbed a staircase without realizing, or, more likely, there were converted basements in the building, because when I got to the end of an empty corridor going off at right angles, which I had hoped would take me back to the yard, where I could run to my dad's arms, I found myself on a kind of platform suspended over a square enclosure divided in two by a grill. With a certain disquiet, I realized I had gone too far. Looking for a way out, in the grip of a horribly familiar panic, I made a crucial mistake: instead of trusting myself to go back the way I had come, I went through the first gap I could find, a gap in the wall, where they must have been doing some kind of renovation: it was a small hole, not much more than a crack, forty centimeters high and twenty wide at the most, at the level of the baseboard. It struck me as the perfect shortcut for getting back to where I had begun. I came out onto a kind of cornice ten meters above the floor. I edged along it with my back to the wall (I was terrified of heights). The roof wasn't far above me. Since I didn't go near the uneven edge, all I could see below was a corridor. It was fairly dark too. The cornice, which in fact was the remains of a plaster ceiling, led to a cubicle, which I crawled into. It was a skylight, about a square meter in cross section, and two or three meters high: at the top, a square of sky. At the base of the walls, level with my feet, were slots opening onto deep, unlighted rooms. Once I was in there, I kept quiet. I sat down on the floor. I thought: I'm going to spend the whole night here. It was four in the afternoon, but for me the night had already begun. I couldn't go any further, because it was a dead end. And it didn't occur to me to go back . . . In that respect I was consistent. Even if my parents didn't always say it, their eternal refrain was "This time you've gone too far." Never "You've come back from too far away," I guess because once you've gone too far there's no way back.

I thought of Dad, mostly to pass the time and stop me from worrying about other things. I multiplied him by all the other men shut in that prison, those desperate men, expelled from society, who couldn't hug their children . . . And there I was on high, hovering over them all . . . I was the angel . . . and it came as no surprise. Each successive incident, right from the start, from the moment I tasted the strawberry ice cream, had been leading me to this crowning moment, preparing me to be the angel, the guardian angel of all the criminals, the thieves and murderers . . .

All the prisoners were my dad, and I loved him. Although I thought I loved him before, when he held me in his arms or led me by the hand, now I knew that love was more, much more than that. I had to become the guardian angel of all the desperate men to discover what love really was.

It was a mystical experience, and it lasted many hours. The experience of intimate contact with humanity as a whole, as only a guardian angel can know it. Not even the fact that I didn't have wings could shake my conviction. On the contrary: wings would have allowed me to get away, up through that square of sky above me.

It was, as I said, a prolonged episode. It lasted all evening and all night. They found me at ten o'clock the next morning. I fantasized about the search provoked by my disappearance, conducted in my absence (knowing how it would end). I could even hear voices calling me; I could hear them coming through the loudspeakers: "César Aira . . . a boy by the name of César Aira." But this was not part of the fantasy, the mental reconstruction. I was meant to respond to those voices. And I wanted to, I wanted to say, for example, "Here I am. Help! I don't know how to get down." But I couldn't. Powerless to act, I could only anticipate future events. I imagined a scene in which I was explaining to the governor of the prison what had really happened: ". . . it was my dad. He grabbed me and hid me somewhere . . . he was going to use me as a hostage in the breakout he's planning with his accomplices . . ." All this was forgivable, even Dad could have forgiven me, considering my innocence, my character, my fears . . . All the same, to ease my conscience, I tried to improve the story: "But Dad was forced to do it, by the King of the Criminals; he would never have chosen to kidnap his own daughter . . ." And then, worried that the governor would get the wrong idea, I added a clarification: "But my Dad isn't the King . . . ." I had embarked on the complex task of lying. The experienced liar knows that the secret of success is to pretend convincingly not to know certain things. For example the consequences of what one is saying, so that others will seem to discover them first. "Not that Dad ever mentioned the King . . . it was the others, they were talking about him, afraid, in awe . . . They were calling Dad your Jamesty . . . I don't know why, because my dad's called Tomás . . ." The governor was bound to fall for my ploy. He would think: It's too complicated not to be true. That's what they always think; it's the golden rule of fiction. He would believe me completely. Not Dad. Dad knew my tricks; he *was* my tricks. He would see through them, but he would forgive me, even if it meant another ten years in jail . . . These were not exactly the reflections of an angel. The sound of the loudspeaker (it was already night, the stars were shining in the sky) swept through the jail, calling me: "Come out of your hiding place, César, your mother is waiting to take you home . . ." Women's voices, the social workers . . . Mom's voice too . . . I even thought I heard Dad's voice—my heart skipped a beat—that beloved voice, which I hadn't heard for so many months, and then I really did wish I had wings to fly away . . . But I couldn't. This was always happening, so often that it literally was the story of my life: hearing a voice, understanding the orders it was giving me, wanting to obey, and not being able to . . . Because reality, the only sphere in which I could have acted, kept withdrawing at the speed of my desire to enter it . . .

In this case, and maybe in all the others too, I had the marvelous consolation of knowing that I was an angel. This knowledge transformed the situation, turning it into a dream, but a real dream. It was a transformation of reality. The cruel delirium I had suffered as a result of the fever was a transformation too, but the opposite kind. In the real dream, reality took the form of happiness or paradise. The transformation could go either way, reality becoming delirium or dream, but the real dream turned dreamlike in turn, becoming the angel, or reality.

7

WINTER CAME, AND MOM began to take in ironing. We spent the interminable evenings inside, listening to the radio, Mom bending over the steaming cloth, me staring at my exercise book, and both of us miles away, our souls meandering in the strangest places. We had adopted an invariable routine. In the morning I went with her to the stores, we had lunch early, she took me to school, came to pick me up at five, and then we stayed in for the rest of the evening. Lured by the radio, we lost ourselves in a labyrinth that I can reconstruct step by step.

Everything in this story I am telling is guaranteed by my perfect memory. My memory has stored away each passing instant. And the eternal instants too, the ones that didn't pass, enclosing the others in their golden capsules. And the instants that were repeated, which of course were the majority.

But my memory merges with the radio. Or rather: I am the radio. Thanks to the faultless perfection of my memory, I am the radio of that winter. Not the receiver, the device, but what came out of it, the broadcast, the continuity, what was being transmitted, even when we switched it off, even when I was asleep or at school. My memory contains it all, but the radio is a memory that contains itself and I am the radio.

Life without the radio was inconceivable for me. What happens, if you decide to define life as radio (which, as an intellectual exercise, is not entirely without merit), is that it automatically produces a sustaining plenitude. It was important for Mom as well, it was company . . . Remember that the disaster had befallen us immediately after our move to Rosario, where we had neither relatives nor friends. And the circumstances were not ideal for making new friends, so Mom was all alone in the world . . . She had her daughter, of course, but even though I was everything to her, that wasn't much. She was a sociable woman who loved to chat . . . So she got to know people in the end, without having to make a particular effort: storekeepers, neighbors, people she did ironing for. They were all keen to hear the story of her recent misfortune, which she told over and over . . . She repeated herself a bit, but that was only natural. Society was destined to absorb her life again;

that winter was a mere interlude . . . The radio fulfilled a function. In her case it was instrumental: it gathered her scattered parts, it reassembled her identity as woman and housewife . . . By contrast I achieved a complete identification with the voices in the ether . . . I embodied them.

Those evenings, those nights in fact, for it grew dark very early, especially in our room, had an atmosphere of shelter and refuge, which was intensely enjoyable, especially for me, I'm not sure why. They were a kind of paradise, which, like all cut-price paradises, had an infernal side. All the ironing Mom had taken in meant that she couldn't go out, but she didn't mind; she was happy in that seeming paradise, contenting herself with appearances, as usual. Her return to society would have to wait. I fastened onto the illusion like a vampire: I lived on the blood of a fantasy paradise.

In this kind of situation, repetition dominates. Each new day is the same as all the others. The radio broadcast was different every day. And yet it was the same. The programs we followed repeated themselves . . . We wouldn't have been able to follow them if they hadn't; we would have lost track. And in the breaks the announcers always read the same advertisements, which I had learned by heart. No surprise there, since memory was, and still is, my forte. I repeated them aloud as they were spoken, one after another. The same with the introductions to the programs and the accompanying music. I shut up when the programs themselves began.

We followed three soap operas. One was about the life of Jesus Christ, or rather the childhood of the God made flesh; it was aimed at children and sponsored by a brand of malt drink, which I had never tasted in spite of the identically repeated panegyrics (with me doubling the speaker's words) celebrating its nutritional and growth-promoting virtues. Jesus and his pals were a likeable gang; there was a black boy, a fat boy, a stammerer and a little giant. The Messiah was the gang leader, and in each episode he performed a mini-miracle, as if he was in training for later life. He wasn't infallible yet and used to get into all sorts of trouble in his efforts to help the poor and the wayward of Nazareth; but things always worked out and, at the end, the deep, resonant voice of God the Father pronounced the moral, if there was one, or some words of wise advice. Those boys became my best friends. I loved their adventures and pranks so much that my imagination worked at top speed, coming up with variations and alternative outcomes; but in the end I always found the scriptwriters' solutions more satisfying. For me it was a kind of reality. A reality that couldn't be seen, only heard, that existed as voices and sounds. It was up to me to provide the images. But within this reality there came a moment—my favorite—when the Father spoke, and at that point everyone, not just me, had to provide an image. God was the radio within the radio.

The second soap opera was historical too, but secular and Argentinean. Entitled *Tell me, Grandma*, it was invari-

ably introduced by a sort of prologue, in which the vener-
able Mariquita Sánchez de Thompson was questioned by
her grandchildren, each time about a different event in
national history to which she had been an eye witness. One
day it would be the first English invasion, another day the
second, or some episode during one or the other, or the
May revolution, a party during the Viceroyalty or the
tyranny of Rosas, an incident in the life of Belgrano or San
Martín . . . I loved the way time was haphazard, the lottery
of the years. I knew nothing about history, of course, but
the preliminary dialogues and the old lady's adorably hesitant voice made me imagine it as a broad expanse of time,
a spread from which to choose . . . And Grandma's memory
seemed to be tenuous, hanging from a thread about to snap
. . . but once she got going, her shaky voice faded, making
way for the actors of the past . . . This substitution was my
favorite part: the voice hesitating among memories and the
mist dissolving to reveal the ultra-real clarity of the scene
as it had happened . . .

Tell me, Grandma was not really aimed at children or at
adults, and yet it was meant for both. It bridged the gap,
reminding adults of what they had learned at school and
acquainting children with things they would remember
when they learned about them. Doña Mariquita and her
grandchildren were as one: she was the eternal little girl . .
. Her failing, aged memory was in fact prodigious: scenes
remote in time came to life not as the past usually does, in
the form of mute images, but images endowed with sound,

every inflection intact, down to the faintest sigh or the sound of chair legs scraping on a sitting-room floor as a viceregal official dead seventy years before stood up suddenly to greet a lady who had lain in her grave for more than half as long, and with whom he was, naturally, in love.

The third soap opera, which started at eight (they were all half an hour long) was definitely for adults. It was about love and featured all the stars of the day. In a sense, this serial connected with reality itself, while the others skirted around it. One proof of this—I saw it as a proof in any case —was the complication of the story. The reality that I knew, my reality, wasn't complicated. On the contrary, it was simplicity itself. It was too simple. I can't summarize the Lux serial as I did with the other two. It didn't have an underlying mechanism; it was pure, free-floating complication. There was a given that guaranteed its perpetual complication: everyone was in love. There were no secondary characters playing supporting roles. Love was the theme of the serial and everyone was in love. They were like molecules with love valencies reaching out into space, into the sonorous ether, and every one of those little yearning arms found a hold. The tangle was so dense, it created a new simplicity: the simplicity of compactness. Space was no longer empty, porous and intangible; it had become a solid rock of love. By contrast, my life was so simple it hardly existed. Deprived as I was, the message I seemed to be receiving from the "radio drama of the stars" was that growing up was a preparation for love, and that only the multitudinous night sky could make a totality, or at least something, out of nothing.

As well as the soap operas, we listened to all sorts of programs: news, quizzes, comedy and, of course, music. Nicola Paone held me spellbound. But I made no distinctions: every piece of music was my favorite, at least while I was listening to it. I even liked tangos, which children usually find boring. The wonderful thing about music for me was the force with which it took control of the present and banished everything else. No matter what melody I was listening to, it seemed the most beautiful in the world, the best, the only one. It was the instant raised to its highest power. The fascination of the present, a kind of hypnotism (yet another!). Again and again I put it to the test: I tried to think of other pieces of music, other rhythms, I tried to compare and remember, but I couldn't; I was flooded by the musical present, captive in a golden jail.

Speaking of music, one day, on Radio Belgrano, in between programs, a singer performed for the first and last time, while Mom and I listened with the utmost attention and not a little perplexity. On this occasion, I think, Mom's attention was equal to mine. No one has ever sung less tunefully than that woman, not even for a joke. No one else with such a bad sense of pitch would have made it to the end of a measure; this woman sang five whole songs, boleros or romantic ballads, to the accompaniment of a piano. Maybe it *was* a joke, I don't know. But it all seemed very serious; the presenter introduced her in a formal manner, and read out the title of each successive song in a lugubrious voice. It was mysterious. Afterwards, they went on with the normal programs, without any kind of comment. Maybe she was a relative of the radio station's owner; maybe she paid for the airtime to treat herself, or to keep a promise. Who knows? Most people would be ashamed to sing like that on their own, under the shower. And she sang on the radio. Maybe she was deaf or otherwise handicapped, and it was a great achievement (but they had neglected to explain this to the listeners). Maybe she could sing well, but she got nervous, though it's hard to believe: it was too bad for that. She couldn't have sung worse if she'd tried. Every note was out of tune, not only the hard ones. It was almost atonal . . . It's inexplicable. It is *the* inexplicable. The mass media provide an ultimate refuge for the truly inexplicable.

Anyway, the inexplicable presence of that singer in some deep recess of my memory, some deep recess of the radio and the universe, is the strangest thing in this book. The strangest thing that has happened to me. The only thing I can't account for. Not that my aim is to explain the tissue of deeply strange events that is my life, but in this case I suspect that an explanation exists, really exists, somewhere in Argentina, in the mind of one of her children, one of her nephews or nieces, or an eye witness . . . Or the mind of the Tone Deaf Singer herself . . . perhaps she is still alive, and remembers, and if she is reading this . . . My number is in the telephone book. My answering machine is always on, but I'm here beside the phone. All you have to do is make yourself known . . . Not by name, of course, your name wouldn't mean anything to me. Sing. Just a few notes will do, a phrase, however short, from any of those songs, and I will certainly recognize you.

8

THE RADIO HELPED ME to live. The repetition that didn't always happen gave me a measure of life: a surprise gift for me to unwrap, mad with joy, as the flow of sound made up its mind whether to be the same or different . . . This calmed my overactive memory . . . I felt I was no longer beginning to live, with the furious cruelty of beginnings, but simply going on with my life . . .

I don't know if this is something that my readers have noticed, but time is always double: one kind of time always conveys another, as its supplement. The time of the radio's live repetitions conveyed the time that was passing. The palanquin carried the elephant. And time really was passing, slowly and majestically. The catastrophe turned out to be a mere possibility, and was left behind. This gave me the impression that there would be no more catastrophes in my life: I would have a life, like everyone else, and look down on catastrophes from the superior vantage point afforded by the consciousness of time . . . and this was what seemed to be happening. At school the teacher went on ignoring me, which was just as well. Mom didn't take me back to the prison. I was in good health. I didn't mind the simplicity of my life. A certain peace had come over me. I was discovering that time, long-term time made of days, weeks and months, and not of horrific moments as before, was operating in my favor. Nothing else was, but that didn't worry me. Time was enough. I clung on to time, and consequently to learning, the only human activity that makes time our ally.

And that is how, for once in my life, I ended up doing something typical of a girl my age: identifying with the teacher. All girls go through a phase of busily giving lessons to their dolls or the imaginary children who inhabit them. How absurd for someone who knows nothing to throw herself so eagerly into teaching. But what a sublime absurdity. What catechisms of feral pedagogy await the perspicacious observer. What lessons in the primacy of action.

As I had no dolls, I had to make do with make-believe children. And as I didn't have any already made up, I used real ones, reimagining them as I pleased. They were my classmates, the only children I knew, and they were ideal for my purposes, because I had no idea of their lives outside school. For me they were absolute schoolchildren. To make the game more fun, I gave them twisted, difficult, baroque personalities. Each one suffered from a different and complicated kind of dyslexia. Being the perfect teacher, I dealt with them individually, attentive to their particular needs, setting tasks adapted to their capacities.

For example . . . In order to explain this game, I have to fall back on examples. This means switching levels, because until now I have managed to avoid the pernicious logic of examples. I'm making a brief exception here solely in the interests of clarity. For example, then, one child's peculiar dyslexia consisted of putting all the vowels together at the beginning of a word, followed by the consonants. He would write the word "consonants" as "ooacnsnnts". That was a relatively simple case. Others got the shapes of the letters wrong, writing them back to front . . . The first example is purely imaginary, no living being has ever been dyslexic in that way; the second is more realistic, but only because it happens to coincide, by pure chance, with a real possibility. I didn't know what dyslexia was; I didn't suffer from it myself, nor did any of my classmates. I had reinvented it all on my own, to make the game more fun. I didn't even suspect that such a disorder might really exist, and would have been surprised to learn that it did.

There were forty-two of us in the class (forty-three including me, but the teacher never included me in the roll-call or acknowledged my presence in any way); so my imaginary class consisted of forty-two children. Forty-two individual cases. Forty-two novels. The idea of leaving even one of them out to lighten the burden would have been inconceivable to me. And the burden was colossal. Because for each kind of dyslexia I had also come up with a unique and appropriate family background and etiology, couched in the somewhat deranged terms at my disposal, but displaying remarkable intuition on the part of a six-year old. For example, in the case of the boy who wrote letters back to front, his dad was a woman and his mom was a man. This affected his performance at school, either because he had to help his mom prepare the meals (being a man, his mom didn't know how to cook), leaving no time for homework, or because the family lived in wretched poverty (his dad, being a woman, couldn't get a proper job). I had to make sure that the cooperative provided the family with stationery, pens, pencils, etc. And every one of the other forty-one cases was just as involved. It was hellishly complicated. No real teacher would have taken on a task of such magnitude.

The situation was aggravated by the inflexible pedagogical principles I had imposed on myself: the complication could never be simplified, it could only progress. Although my system of teaching was labyrinthine (because of the number of students), it was a one-way labyrinth, with valves all facing in the same direction. The idea wasn't to correct each student's dyslexia, not at all. I wanted to teach them to read and write on their own terms, each according to his particular hieroglyphic system: only within that system was progress possible. For example, the boy who wrote back to front might begin by writing the word *mother* that way and go on to write a thousand-page back-to-front book, a dictionary, anything. I hadn't invented disorders so much as systems of difficulty. They weren't destined to be cured but developed. I'm using the word "dyslexia" here only because the condition is familiar and happens to bear a purely formal resemblance to my systems.

I would read out a dictation passage (in my head, of course, in imagination) then I would collect the (also imaginary) exercise books, and with that absolute honesty only to be observed among children at play, I conscientiously examined forty-two hieroglyphic texts, correcting each according to its unique and nontransferable rule.

As if that wasn't enough, for each kind of dyslexia I also had to determine as best I could how it would affect the student's performance in subjects other than Spanish: Mathematics, Physical Education, Drawing, and so on. To use the simplest example again (others were far more complex), the boy who wrote back to front not only counted using numbers written backwards, but also reversed the functions, so that two plus two made zero, and two minus two made four; the Argentinean nationalists demanded a *closed* meeting of the council in May 1810, Columbus discovered Europe, the fruit came before the flower; as for his drawings, I had to imagine them.

I had to imagine everything, because I gave my classes without props or materials of any kind, not even a piece of paper to take notes on (in any case, at that early stage in my stumbling education I wrote so slowly that there was no way I could have taken notes on the fly, like a stenographer, and I had to keep moving quickly in order to make any progress with so many students). I did it sitting still, concentrating hard, with my eyes open, and some idle part of my mind listening to the radio. My house of cards was always on the point of collapsing; the slightest distraction and I could lose the thread irretrievably. A diagram would have been my salvation. I came to long for a diagram. Had I been able to play aloud it wouldn't have been so hard, but I didn't, because secrecy was essential to the game's aesthetic. So Mom never knew that I was giving lessons. What can she have thought, seeing me sitting there frozen stiff, still as a statue . . .

I had to fall back on a mnemonic system. My memory was perfect, but it wasn't enough. I had gotten myself into a situation where I needed something more. I needed a method, and my method made use of an image of the classroom full of children. To compose this image I needed the figures to be still and silent. Now, in that classroom, and I suppose it would be the same with any class of forty-two six-year-olds (not counting me), it was rare for all the children to be sitting quietly in their places. The only time it happened, in fact, was when the teacher read out the roll. It was like a litany, first the surname, then the first name (mine, which should have come second, between Abate and Artola, was missing). By dint of repetition, I had learned the roll by heart. And in my mind it was like the soundtrack for the mental image of the classroom, each child in his place like a memory peg . . . Unfortunately the combination meant I couldn't use the image in a straight-forward way, because the alphabetical order of the children's names on the soundtrack didn't coincide with the order of their places in the room. So I was forced to zigzag laboriously; one order was superimposed on the other . . .

I found this pastime absorbing. So absorbing that it began to give me pleasure, the first lasting and governable pleasure of my life. It was an aching, almost overwhelming pleasure—that's just the way I was. And soon it underwent a sublimation, transcending itself . . . Almost independently of my will, it created a supplement, which my imagination seized upon with a mad voracity. I transcended school. I began to give instructions. Instructions for everything, for life. I gave them to no one, to impalpable beings within my personality, who didn't even take imaginary forms. They were no one and they were everyone.

The instructions I gave could refer to anything at all. In principle, they were instructions for something I was doing, but they could also be for an activity in which I was not and would never be engaged (such as scaling a moun-tain peak), which didn't stop me prescribing a method for it in the minutest detail. But mainly my instructions referred to what I happened to be doing; that was the default case, the model. It got to the point where every-thing I did was doubled by instructions for doing it.

Activities and instructions were indistinguishable. If I was walking I would also be instructing a ghostly disciple in how to walk, the best method for walking . . . It wasn't as simple as it looked, nothing was . . . Because true efficiency was a kind of elegance, and elegance required minutely detailed knowledge, so detailed it was peculiar to me, an esoteric idiosyncrasy that only I could pass on . . . though to whom, I didn't know, maybe no one, but then again . . . The game took over my life. How to hold a fork, how to raise it to one's mouth, how to take a sip of water, how to look out the window, how to open a door, how to shut it, how to switch on the light, how to tie one's shoelaces . . . Everything accompanied by an unbroken flow of words: "Do it like this . . . never do it like that . . . once I did it like this . . . be careful to . . . some people prefer to. . . this way the results are not so. . ." It was a rapid flow, very rapid, with never a pause for me to catch my breath, because keeping up the pace was essential to getting it right, and I was setting an example. There were so many activities for which I had to issue instructions . . . no end to them . . . and some were simultaneous: glancing slightly to the right at a point just above the horizon, controlling the movement of the eyes and the head (and this glance had to be accompanied by some elegant and appropriate thought, or it would be worthless!), at the same time as picking up a little stone with a precise movement of the fingers . . . How to manipulate cutlery, how to put on one's trousers, how to swallow saliva. How to keep still, how to sit on a chair, how to breathe! I was doing yoga without knowing it, hyper-yoga . . . But it wasn't an exercise for me: it was a class. I took it for granted that I already knew everything, I had mastered it all . . . that's why it was my duty to teach . . . And I really did know it all, naturally I did, since the knowledge was life itself unfolding spontaneously. Although the main thing was not knowing, or even doing, but explaining, opening out the folds of knowledge . . . And so curious are the mechanisms of the mind and language, that sometimes I surprised myself in the role of pupil, receiving my own instructions.

9

MOM WAS MY BEST friend. It wasn't one of those choices that defines a personality, or any other sort of choice, but a necessity. We were alone, isolated. What did we have left to cling to but each other? In such cases we make a virtue of necessity, which doesn't mean it's any less virtuous. Or any less necessary. Our necessity wasn't deep, it didn't have roots or ramifications. It was a casual, provisional necessity. It would be hard to find two beings with fewer affinities than Mom and I. We weren't even complementary opposites, because we were alike. She was a dreamer too. She would have preferred to hide it from me, but some tiny sign gave her away. Our secret personalities are revealed by furtive actions, but they were what I noticed first of all, so poor Mom had no hope of pretending with me. My monstrous, piercing eyes prevented any living being from merging into the background of my life.

Nevertheless, I made a friend that year: a boy, a neighbor, we played together, a friend in the normal sense of the word . . . I was becoming almost a normal little girl, in the normal sense of the word (the word "normal" that is). But no, that's going too far. The story of my friendship with Arturo Carrera is peculiar in the extreme.

We lived, as I think I've already said, in a run-down tenement in a poor neighborhood of Rosario, near the river. We occupied a single room, one of the better ones, as it happened, on the top floor. Places like that are normally swarming with children, but the owners of the building didn't allow them. They had made an exception for me because I was an only child, because Mom was desperate and, above all, because she told them I was mentally retarded, which was believable given my appearance. There must have been some more complicated reason why they made an exception for Arturo Carrera, but I've never tried to get to the bottom of it. (Although it's the key to everything.)

He had lost his father and his mother; his only living relative was his grandma, and she in turn had no one else but him. The same situation as Mom and me, but much more so: we were temporarily alone in Rosario; they were definitively alone in the world. Also their relationship was not at all like ours, since they were so different from us. The grandmother was very old, as small as a child, with white hair and a black dress. She spoke a Sicilian dialect and no one except her grandson could understand her. Nevertheless, she went out and did the shopping on her own, and talked with all the neighbors. I don't know how she managed.

As for Arturito, he was very small for his age. He was seven, a year older than me, but his head didn't even come up to my shoulder, and I wasn't tall. He had a very pale, waxy complexion and blond hair, which he slicked back with oil. But what really made it obvious that he didn't have a mother or a father or aunts or anything were his clothes. Any reasonable adult would have made him dress in a manner more suited to his age. As it was, he could indulge his whims. He wore suits, with starched white shirts, cufflinks and ties; sometimes they were three-piece suits with a waistcoat, or a checked sports jacket with grey flannel trousers, and claret-colored moccasins buffed to a high polish. He looked like a dwarf. His taste in fabrics and cuts was appalling, but that was nothing compared to the fabulous incongruity of wearing that *kind* of attire. And yet, it has to be said that he didn't attract too much attention. Perhaps the people in the tenement and the neighborhood had gotten used to him. Perhaps those ridiculous outfits suited the kind of kid he was. He had a strong personality, you had to give him that. And perhaps the price he had to pay for it was the incongruity of his clothes. By contrast I had no personality. I was prepared to pay the price, but I couldn't imagine what it might be. As well as being impossible for financial reasons, imitating Arturito wouldn't have done me any good, although there was no one else I could have taken as a model. So I gave up the idea of imitating him and having a personality, dimly intuiting that my only hope of being someone lay in this renunciation. I became anxious. I looked at myself in the mirror and couldn't find a single distinctive feature. I was invisible. I was the girl in the crowd. Without a moment's hesitation, I would have exchanged my regular, pretty features for Arturito's nose . . .

No portrait of my friend could be complete without a mention of his most salient feature, that enormous hooked nose of his, so huge it gave form to his whole face, projecting it forward. Another notable characteristic was his voice. Or rather, his way of talking, as if his mouth had been pumped full of gas or stuffed with a hot potato. This gave him an affected, ruling-class sort of air, indescribable but not inimitable. Nothing is inimitable.

Arturito considered himself rich. He thought he was worth a fortune. As the last and only scion of a family of wealthy landowners, he would logically inherit all the properties and the income they yielded . . . But this was sheer fantasy. He and his grandmother were extremely poor. They barely scraped by with what she earned from odd sewing jobs, and Arturito's sartorial expenses were ruining her. It was odd that he persisted so unshakably in his conviction, when all she ever talked about was how wretchedly short of money they were and her fears for the future: if she died he could end up begging on the streets. It's true that she said all this in her dialect, and nobody apart from him could understand. But since he understood, how could he ignore what she was saying and what it meant for him: precisely that he *wasn't* rich. He let her words wash over him. As if she was playing to the gallery, complaining to the others, who couldn't understand her!

In spite of these peculiarities, or because of them, Arturito was a happy child, one of those non-existent typical children, immune to the characteristic torments of middle-class childhood, of which I was such a striking exemplar. He didn't have a care in the world. Extremely sociable and popular, always at the forefront of fashion, he was in his element at school. The only reason I got to know him was that we happened to live in the same building, otherwise I would never have had access to his magic circle. He became my protector, my agent, always praising my intelligence to the skies. Like everything else about him, his courtesy was over the top. He never missed an opportunity to celebrate my virtues, the towering superiority of my intellect relative to his . . . And perhaps he was right, without realizing. For a start, I kept my inner life to myself, while he revealed his. Concealment means you have something to conceal. I had nothing but concealed it anyway, stepping onto the world's stage like someone who has just buried a treasure. I couldn't believe how lucky I was to be best friends with the most popular boy in the school, but even this incredulity was duplicitous. For a start, I was careful to conceal it from Arturito. And then I didn't follow his example in matters of style. He was no help to me in that regard. The hallucinatory style of which I was the supreme mistress remained pristine within me, immune to his influence or any other. Style-wise, Arturito represented another world, the world of wealth . . . His hallucination threw mine into relief . . . being rich meant jumping to a whole new level, beyond style, precision and refinement: life became one radiant, compact mass, without the halftones and subtle differential movements that gave my life sense. So without really meaning to, without malice, I concealed myself entirely from Arturito. I concealed a small part of myself and that part concealed the rest . . . I betrayed my one, irreplaceable friend. How could I have done it? I don't know. Or maybe I do. It was as if I had put on a mask, to shield the twists and turns of an ever-changing subject.

A fantasy particularly dear to Arturito's heart revolved around the fancy dress parties, the grand masquerades he supposedly organized for his innumerable friends every year at carnival time. It sounded flippant at first, but he went on to talk about the parties with absolute conviction and he had a fund of stories about things that had happened in previous years. Mom and I had moved into the tenement just after carnival and there was still a while to go before it came round again, so I had no way of knowing if there was any truth to these stories or not. For Arturito life without fancy dress parties was simply inconceivable. He seemed to be perpetually dressed for one, in those little suits of his. Although it was barely the beginning of spring, he was already thinking about the costume he would wear to the next carnival party, to which I had already been invited . . . if I would deign to attend, if I would do him that honor, if I would condescend to partake briefly of frivolities so unworthy of me . . .

He didn't seem very imaginative. He wasn't, compared to me. Or rather he was too imaginative; again he went a bit too far (for my taste), and ended up in a kind of radiant mist of excessive imagining that enabled him to be happy—that is, rich, aristocratic, carefree—but which also sapped the imagination's creative vigor. He had got it into his head to wear an astronomer's costume to the next party. Just what this costume might consist of, he couldn't say. For him it was just a word: "astronomer", and its train of associations, spellbinding or, as he loved to say, "exquisite" things, like stars, constellations, galaxies . . .

But when he asked me what I was going to wear, although I had a thousand times more imagination than him, I couldn't come up with an answer.

So he decided to help me. It was in the afternoon, after school but before the soap operas. We were in the tenement courtyard, and silence had settled around us, one of those dead silences that attends exclusively on children as they plumb the depths of the day. He told me he had something I could use; although it wasn't a costume, it might be a starting point . . . He disappeared into his room. The silence persisted. His grandmother was perfectly quiet . . . It was like the silence when everyone is sleeping, but it wasn't siesta time: it was a coincidence. I was worried, uneasy: Arturito was so impulsive, so wrapped up in his own world . . . What would he come back with? He might offend me without meaning to. I had a twinge of dread, but it didn't last long. I trusted to my impassivity, which was supernatural.

There was no need to be worried. All he came back with was a cardboard nose. He had used it for one of the jokes he was always playing . . . His philosophy began and ended with the idea that a busy social life could only be fuelled by large quantities of humor, and humor, as he understood it, consisted of practical jokes, the sort that are funny to look back on. It was just a nose, huge though it was, with an elastic band to hold it on . . . A nose as big as his or bigger . . . with the same shape . . . I was overcome by an infantile enthusiasm. Was it for me? Naturally, it went without saying. Sometimes Arturito was wildly generous. And sometimes he was maniacally stingy. He was so contradictory. He fastened it to my face himself. Not that he thought I was clumsy . . . no, but because of my alleged superiority I was unaccustomed to carrying out mundane tasks. The nose suited me perfectly. He looked at me and said that I was already half way there. I had the rudiments or the trimmings of a costume, it was just a matter of supplementing it now . . . with one of my mother's old dresses . . . Suddenly he became enthusiastic too, or maybe I just hadn't noticed it before . . . In any case his enthusiasm began to turn on him . . . I could see it coming. We were six and seven years old respectively, and seized by an absolute urgency . . . as if the party were to be held that night . . . The supernatural silence reigning in the building had abolished time. Arturito had another idea and ran back into his room . . . He came back clacking something in his hand. His grandmother's porcelain false teeth. I wasn't surprised that he'd been able to steal them; she didn't wear them all the time . . . The clack-clack sound he was making resonated in the silence, that silence in which anything could be stolen . . . It was obvious, really: the teeth had to go with the nose. He wanted me to try them . . . but of course I refused . . . there was no way I was putting *that* in my mouth, nothing that had been in someone else's mouth was going to enter mine . . . So he tried the false teeth himself. They distorted his face, especially when he smiled . . . I could tell what was coming: now he would want the nose . . . Instinctively, I raised my hands to protect it. In his innocence he mentioned the Astronomer; he wanted to be the Astronomer with false teeth and a fake nose . . . If he had asked me, I would have given the nose back to him without the slightest hesitation . . . But no, there was a second turn: his generosity triumphed and at the same time transcended itself . . . he would hang the false teeth around my neck with a thread. I would be a Cannibal . . . Or better still: the nose hanging around my neck and the teeth as a barrette in my hair . . . or the nose growing out of my chest and the teeth in my armpit . . . There was a moment of

sheer permutation, nose and teeth shifting positions all over
my body ... It had to happen eventually ... maybe I had
the idea first, or he did, impossible to tell, it was like a scientific discovery ... The cardboard nose had to go on my
nose, that was the natural place for it ... And the teeth had
to bite it ... It was a costume in itself: the little girl bitten
by a ghost ... The ghost opened a breach in time, so it did-
n't matter that carnival was still six months away ... With
one bite he placed the false teeth at the perfect angle ...
Some improvisations outstrip any art ... he sank his teeth
into the cardboard, without taking the nose off me ... I was
worried about him ruining his fake nose, but Arturito was
not so much generous as sacrificial; he would destroy his
possessions with the indifference of a millionaire for the
sake of a laugh or a bit of fun ... Those little porcelain teeth
felt like rat's teeth, razor sharp ... I didn't know they were
porcelain, I though they were from a dead person, I
thought that's where false teeth came from; that's what lots
of people think ... The teeth went through the cardboard
... Arturito laughed until he cried; he was fashioning me
with that deft clumsiness of his ... I wanted to see myself
in a mirror ... although I didn't really need to; I could see
myself in my friend's little grey eyes ... it was phenomenal
... the girl who had been bitten by a ghost ... But in his
passion, the passion for fancy dress that ruled his life,
Arturito went too far. He bit too hard. The dentures—and
suddenly the full horror of those cadaver's teeth was
revealed to me—cut into my nose ... because my real nose

was there beneath Arturito's cardboard fake . . . It wasn't so much the pain as the surprise . . . I had forgotten about having a body of flesh and blood, but now, bitten, suffocating, terrified, I remembered . . . I let out a spine-chilling scream . . . I was sure he had mutilated me; now I would be a monster, a skull . . . Arturito recoiled in horror. My expression froze the blood in his veins . . . he would never forget this . . . but it would become an amusing anecdote, one more to add to his stock, perhaps the best, the funniest . . . although for the moment he was dumbfounded . . . He looked at me and I looked at myself in his terrified eyes, as I wriggled free of his grip and ran away . . . as fast as I could, in panic . . . Where was I going? Where was I running to? If only I had known! I was running away from jokes, from humor and future anecdotes . . . I was running away from friendship, and not because I disdained it or had something more important to do, as Arturito thought, in his innocence: it was pure, darkest horror that gave my feet wings.

10

ALL THAT HAD HAPPENED had helped to make time pass. Suddenly, in spite of my habitual distraction, I noticed that the consistency of the air was changing: it wasn't as cold, the days were getting longer . . . Spring was coming. It was as if the year was receding into the past, compacted into a block of dead matter, foreign to me. It was absorbing all the little differences, the movements, tremors and thoughts, extracting them from the present, making way, I sensed, for something new and heady and slightly wild. Not that I let optimism get the better of me—my experience was too unilateral for that, and anyway it wouldn't have been my style. It was more the sense of a cycle coming to a close, but since my life had begun, as it were, that autumn, shortly after our arrival in Rosario, I didn't see the cycle from the outside, as a repetition, but from the inside, as a rectilinear movement. In short, I had the feeling that things were about to change.

And how could it have been otherwise, since the world around me was changing, and I was changing myself? I was no longer preoccupied by school, or Dad's absence, or the teacher's campaign against me, or the radio, or Arturito. It was as if everything had worn thin and become transparent . . . I clung to that transparence, but without anxiety or pain, as if I wasn't clinging but moving freely through it, like a bird. I felt the pull of open spaces, like those I had known in Pringles, although I had no memory of Pringles; a total amnesia cut me off from my life before Rosario, before the invention of my memory. But the spaces of Pringles were not a memory. They were a desire, a kind of happiness that could exist anywhere: all I had to do was open my eyes, hold out my hand . . .

That space, that happiness had a color: rose-pink. The pink of the sky at sunset, a vast, transparent, faraway pink whose absurd apparition represented my life. I was vast, transparent and faraway, and my absurd life represented the sky. Living was painting: coloring myself with the pink of the inexplicably suspended light . . .

In our neighborhood, the houses were low, the streets broad, and the pageants of the sky were within arm's reach. Mom started letting me go to school on my own—it was four blocks away. I dawdled, especially on the way home, as dusk unfolded. I was coming to know freedom and aim-lessness. I was discovering the city . . . without actually going into it, of course . . . I kept to my far-flung corner and imagined the rest of the city from there, and especially from the riverbank, where I went every day to have a look around, because it wasn't far and there was always a chance to get out of the house. Of course I never let a chance go by. I accompanied Mom on all her errands . . . I always had, because she didn't dare leave me alone in the room, imagining all sorts of disasters, I guess. But now I had come up with a specially fun method of accompanying her. I had to turn every pleasure into a vice, a mania. There were no half measures with me. Mom had to resign herself to it, although it was a constant source of problems and worries. What I did was to "tail" her. I'd let her get ahead, a hundred meters or so, while I hid, and then I'd follow her, remaining hidden, going from tree to tree, doorway to doorway . . . I hid (it was sheer love of fiction on my part, because she soon wearied of the game and stopped turning around to look) behind anything that would afford me cover: a parked car, a lamp post, a pedestrian . . . When she turned a corner, I ran and hid behind it, spying on her, letting her get ahead again, waiting for a new opportunity to sneak up on her under cover . . . If I saw her go into a store, I'd wait in hiding, my eyes fixed on the door . . . When she went back home, it was an anticlimax. I'd wait for half an hour on the corner to see if she was going to come out again, and then, finally, I'd go in, usually to be greeted with a slap; my ruses had understandably frayed her nerves. I almost always lost her. I tried to be too clever, made it unnecessarily hard, to the point where the distance between us was neither short nor long, because it had simply evaporated. Then I would go home and hide in the hallway, not knowing if she had come back or not . . . and sometimes she had to cut short her shopping and come home, when it became obvious that I wasn't following her . . . Then she would give me a slap and go out again, dragging me by the hand this time, squeezing it until the bones cracked . . . I was incorrigible. The game was my freedom. Oddly, while I was playing it, I never issued any of my famous mental instructions, although the game would have been perfect for them . . . I guess my tailing was already, in itself, a series of instructions, and maps, for making a city . . . Mom stayed within a fairly small radius around our home: always the same streets, the same routes, the grocery store, the butcher's, the fishmonger's, the fruit and vegetable store . . . There was no danger of me getting lost. I always lost track of her sooner or later, but I didn't get lost myself. Although she never stopped fearing that I would. And neither of us would have been surprised if I had. I can't understand why I never did.

What I couldn't work out was how I managed to lose her, how she eluded my tenacious, lucid pursuit; it should have been simple to tail her, the simplest task in the world. Subconsciously I knew that the last thing Mom wanted was for me to lose sight of her. It was only in my game that she was a wily criminal who noticed the ingenious detective on her trail, and threw her off, or tried to, with cunning ploys . . . Poor Mom must have wished she could walk me on a leash . . . but since she couldn't stop me hiding in a doorway until she got a certain distance ahead, all she asked was that I stay within sight of her. She would gladly have left a trail of breadcrumbs or buttons, or made herself phosphorescent or carried a flag on a pole, so her idiotic daughter wouldn't lose her again . . . But she couldn't. She couldn't make herself too obvious, because that would have meant she was playing my game. It would have been easy for her to walk slowly in the middle of the sidewalk, remaining clearly visible, stopping for a minute at every corner, or before entering a store . . . That way she could have been sure that I was still following her. But she couldn't play my game. It's not that she didn't want to; she *couldn't*. It was almost a question of life or death. She couldn't grant me that importance. Nor, of course, could she make it hard for me by hiding, shaking me off straight away, which would have been a cinch, but it was doubly impossible because her maternal instinct would have made her sick with worry. The only option left was to act naturally, to do her shopping as if she was on her own, as if no one was following her . . . But she couldn't do that either! That was the most impossible thing of all. How could she act naturally, with my eyes boring into her back, when she knew perfectly well I was a hundred meters behind her, hidden behind a dog or a trash can? So where did that leave her? All she could do was combine the three impossibilities, unable to settle on any of them, bouncing from one to another.

Encouraged by my failures (let others be encouraged by success!), I started making it even more difficult. Instead of a distance of a hundred meters, I made it two hundred. I lost sight of her at once. The tailing was no longer visual but divinatory. This was a natural extension of my habit of giving instructions, which had ended up informing my relation to the world; everything had to be done with the utmost subtlety and finesse . . . The fact that I failed was secondary. The methodical imperative came first. Also, this way, the sense of pursuit was stronger, more intense . . . to the point where it all flipped around. When I lost Mom— and, increasingly, I made sure that this happened at the beginning of the outing—I started to feel that *I* was being tailed.

This feeling grew exponentially. I had the brilliant idea of telling Mom about it. My rashness was breathtaking. At first she paid no attention, but I insisted just enough to get her worried, before backing off. So many dreadful things had been happening . . . She asked me if I'd seen who was following me, if it was a man or a woman . . . I didn't know how to explain that it wasn't like that, I was talking about feelings, subtleties, "instructions."

"You're not going out any more unless I've got you by the hand!"

Around that time the gutter press was feasting on the

bloodless cadavers of boys and girls, found raped in vacant lots . . . They had been completely drained of blood. A vampire plague was sweeping the land. Mom was a village girl, and though not completely ignorant (she had done a year of secondary school), she was naïve, easily taken in . . . So different from me! She not only believed what she read in the gutter press (if it came to that, I probably did too), but applied it to her own real life. That was the key difference, the abyss that separated us. I had a real life completely separate from beliefs, from the common reality made up of shared beliefs . . .

Anyway, once, during one of our outings . . . I had completely lost Mom, and I didn't know whether to keep going straight, or turn, or go back home (it was only two blocks away).

The thing was, we had just set out; Mom wouldn't be back for a good half hour, and she'd be nervous and worried about me, and maybe cross because she couldn't finish her shopping . . .

A strange woman accosted me. "Hello, César."

She knew my name. I didn't know anyone and no one knew me. Where was she from? Maybe she lived in the tenement, or worked in one of the stores where Mom did her shopping. To me all ladies looked the same, so she could have been anyone, and I wasn't too surprised not to be able to recognize her. The really strange thing was that she had spoken to me. Because it wasn't just a question of her identity, but also, and above all, of mine. I was so convinced of my own invisibility, of the utter ordinariness of my features, that I felt this could only be a miracle. It must have something to do with the marks on my nose, I thought, raising my hand to touch them.

"What happened to your little nose?" she asked with interest, smiling.

"I got bitten," I said, without going into details, not because I didn't want to tell her the whole story (I promised myself I would, eventually), but to be polite, not to bore her, not to waste her time.

"How awful! Was it a friend, a naughty boy? Or a doggy?"

Her insistence annoyed me. It showed that she hadn't appreciated my politeness. I was impatient to change the subject, to get things clear between us; then I would be able to tell her the story of the bite in graphic detail. I shrugged my shoulders impatiently, with a faint smile.

As if she had read my mind, she changed tack. "Do you remember me?"

I nodded, with the same smile, but a little more relaxed and charming now. She gave a visible start, but regained control immediately. She smiled again, more broadly. "Do you really remember?"

I had said yes simply to be polite, to reciprocate, since she knew me.

I nodded again, but this time the nod had a totally different meaning. I wasn't exactly sure what that meaning was, though I could make a vague guess at it. This woman didn't know me at all, in fact. She was lying. She was a kid-napper, a vampire . . . But guessing always involves a mar-gin of uncertainty. And operating from that margin, polite-ness and polite circumspection took control of everything. Even if I had believed that vampires really existed, they wouldn't have scared me as much as the prospect of upset-ting the status quo. Politeness was a kind of stability or bal-ance. For me, life depended on it. Giving it up would have to be worse that being preyed on by a vampire. Anyway, I didn't believe in vampires, and this lady wasn't one. So by nodding, what I meant was that nothing had changed.

"No, you don't remember, but it doesn't matter. I'm a friend of your mother's, but I haven't seen her for a long time. We knew each other in Pringles . . . How is she?"

"Very well."

"And Don Tomás?"

"He's in jail."

"Yes, I heard."

She was an ordinary woman, a bottle blonde, rather short and stout, very smartly dressed . . .

There was something hysterical and delirious about her. I could feel it in the intensity of the scene. It wasn't how someone would normally talk to a little girl they had met by chance in the street. It was as if she had rehearsed it, as if, for her, a fundamental drama was unfolding. It did-n't worry me too much because there are people like that, women especially, for whom every moment has the same tragic intensity, without any kind of emotional relief.

"What are you doing out on your own? Are you running an errand?"

"Yes."

She looked at me in surprise. My yeses shattered all her preconceptions. Then she went for broke. "Do you want to come to my house? I live just nearby; you can have some cookies . . ."

"I don't know . . ."

Suddenly reality, the reality of the kidnapping, hit me. And I wasn't prepared for it. I couldn't believe it. My politeness was sheer idiocy. For the sake of manners, I was giving up everything, even my life. From that moment on I was seized by an immense fear. But the fear remained hidden beneath my manners. Wasn't that typical? Any other reaction would have amazed me.

"I'll take you back home afterwards. I want to say hello to your Mom, it's so long since I've seen her." She anticipated my answer with an intensity multiplied a thousandfold.

"Ah, all right then," I said theatrically, exaggerating my willingness. It was the least I could do, to thank her for making an effort to clear away the impediments.

She took me by the hand and dragged me briskly along the Avenida Brown. She talked all the time but I wasn't listening. Anxiety was suffocating me. When she looked at me, I smiled at her. I fell in with her step and returned the pressure of her hand on mine. I thought that by stressing my willingness, I was making the hypothesis of a kidnapping too far-fetched. In no time at all we were on a bus, going down unfamiliar streets. The bus was half empty, but she spoke up so all the passengers could hear; she kept cuddling me and saying my name: César, César, César. I loved it when people said my name; it was my favorite word.

"Do you remember when you were little, César, and I used to take you for ice cream?"

"Yes."

I was lying. I was lying. I had never eaten ice cream in my life!

I played along with her act, anticipating, waiting . . . I took politeness to the clearly absurd extreme of supposing that she had mixed me up with another girl, who had the same name as me, had been born in Pringles and whose father was in prison . . . In which case, she would be so disappointed when she found out the truth . . . she might even get angry, because my yeses would turn out to have been lies, excesses of politeness.

We got off in a distant, unfamiliar neighborhood, and walked a couple of blocks, holding hands all the way . . . But her mask was beginning to crack, the madness she had been laboriously keeping under control was rising to the surface, tinged with violence and sarcasm. I felt obliged to accentuate my politeness, to guard against an imminent collapse.

"Mom's going to be so happy to see you!"

"Yes, she'll be thrilled."

"What a lovely neighborhood!"

"Do you like it, Cesitar?"

"Yes."

Her voice had become so sinister! My diagnosis was incontrovertible: this woman was crazy. You would have to be crazy to give up an imaginary status quo. You would have to be crazy to prefer brute reality. I tried not to think about being at the mercy of a crazy woman. Anyway, what could she do to me?

We arrived. She unlocked the front door and shut it again behind us. The house was old and half derelict. Still holding me by the hand (she turned the key and the door handle with her left hand, not letting me go for a moment), she led me down a hallway and through some dark rooms, quickly, without speaking. I was trying to think of something nice to say, but before I could, we were in a sitting room at the back of the house. There were no windows, so she switched on the light. We had arrived. She let me go and took two steps back. She stared at me with fire in her eyes.

She took off the mask and revealed her witch's face . . . But there was no need, I had already unmasked her with my politeness. Having striven so hard, in vain, to convince me of one thing, now she wanted to convince me of the opposite. After her superhuman efforts to persuade me that she was good . . . Now she wanted to persuade me that she was bad . . . But the switch wasn't going to be that easy. My strategy had blocked the movement of belief in both directions.

"Do you know who I am?"

Affirmative smile.

"Do you know who I am, you little moron?"

Affirmative smile.

"Do you know who I am, you stupid brat? I'm the wife of the ice-cream vendor, the one your brute of a father killed. His widow! *That's* who I am!"

"Ah." Another affirmative smile. I couldn't believe my own stubbornness: I was still trying to keep up the act. But all things considered, it was the most logical option. If I had come this far, I could keep going indefinitely.

"I've been watching you for months, you and your goody-goody mother. You're not going to get away with it. Eight years they gave him, that animal, eight lousy years! And he killed my poor husband; he killed him . . ."

At this point, without meaning to, I was supremely impolite. I smiled, shrugged my shoulders and said, "I don't understand . . ."

I understood very well what was happening. I understood what vengeance was; I think that was about all I did understand. But the only way for me to maintain my polite temper was to feign naivety and ignorance of all those grown-up things beyond my understanding. Perhaps because I sensed that this was my last chance to make politeness work, I channeled all my natural acting talent into that shrug and those words. I was perfect. That was my downfall. I could have saved myself simply by saying something else, anything. She would have stopped to think; she would have reconsidered the terrible vendetta that she was about to execute . . . After all she was a woman, she had a heart, she could be moved; I was a perfectly innocent six-year old girl, I wasn't guilty of anything and deep down she knew it . . . But my "I don't understand" was so perfect that it drove her completely wild, it blinded her. And my imperturbably polite smile ("Whatever you say, Ma'am") was the last straw. It stripped her of tragedy, of explanation, and at that moment explanation was all she had left.

She said nothing more. The sitting room was cluttered with metal containers and equipment: what was left of the ice-cream store. She had it all planned. She switched on a little motor (the wiring was makeshift; this set-up only had to work once) and as well as its buzzing I could hear the glug-glug of ice cream being mixed. She looked into an aluminum drum, threw the lid to the floor and switched off the motor . . . She put in her hand and scooped up a handful of strawberry ice cream, which came dribbling out between her fingers . . .

"Would you like some?"

I was paralyzed, but I could feel my wooden automaton preparing an ultimate "affirmative smile," in spite of everything! . . . And that was the supreme horror . . . Luckily she didn't give me time. She jumped on me, swept me up like a doll . . . I didn't resist, I was rigid . . . She hadn't wiped her hand and I felt a cold tickle in my armpit as the ice cream seeped through my shirt. She took me to the drum and threw me in head first . . . The drum was big, I was tiny, and since the ice cream wasn't very hard, I managed to right myself and touch the bottom with my feet. But she put the lid on before I could get my head out, and screwed it down onto the overflowing contents. I held my breath because I knew I wouldn't be able to breathe submerged in ice cream . . . The cold seeped into my bones . . . My little heart beat fit to burst . . . I knew, I who had never known anything in reality, that this was death . . . And my eyes were open; by a strange miracle I saw the pink that was killing me: luminous, too beautiful to bear . . . I must have been seeing it not with my eyes but with my frozen optic nerves: a strawberry eye scream . . . My lungs exploded with a rasping pain, my heart contracted for the last time and stopped . . . my brain, most loyal of my organs, kept working for a moment longer, just long enough for me to think that what was happening to me was death, real death . . .

26th of February 1989